ACT OF LOVE

ACT OF LOVE

Joe R. Lansdale

Carroll & Graf Publishers, Inc.
New York

Originally published by CD Publications.

This edition published by arrangement with the author.

First Carroll & Graf edition 1995.

Carroll & Graf Publishers, Inc.
260 Fifth Avenue
New York, NY 10001

ISBN 0-7867-0288-5

Manufactured in the United States of America.

10   9   8   7   6   5   4   3   2   1

To Mary Louise Lansdale and my wife, Karen

FOREWORD

Andrew Vachss

If you're looking for cute, keep moving—I consider this opportunity an honor, and I'm not about to squander it on air-pumped hyperbole.

Writing the foreword to a significant piece of work has but one rule: tell the truth. It's not a job for a blurb-meister. If you want adjectives, visit the paperback rack at your local airport. If Joe wanted some stream-of-consciousness, thesaurus-busting river of praise, he would have asked someone else.

But Joe doesn't play . . . not that way.

"Genre" writing is an endangered species . . . for all the reasons any species starts to run out of road. Overpopulation, in-breeding, lack of natural predators, limited food supply. Words don't work as stand-alones: they gather their power from juxtaposition . . . from context, from precision placement. But, in our game, words have become devalued currency—you can't count on them anymore. Our field is overdosed with flab: take some gratuitous,

ANDREW VACHSS

implausible violence, throw in some unrealistic sex, splatter some guts and hair on the nearest wall, sprinkle in a touch of mystical reference . . . and you're walking the "dark" side.

Sure.

The genres . . . horror, crime, fantasy, whatever . . . all have their built-in places to hide. Write something stupid, it's a metaphor. Write something mean-spirited and small, it's satire.

Spare me. Skeletons charging out of closets isn't my idea of liberation.

The real monsters aren't in basements, they're in families, incubating. In parishes and prisons, drive-ins and day-care centers . . . waiting their time.

They're not "fiction" either.

Getting published is pretty easy today. And that's good. I'm all for an open admissions policy. But the sorting-out phase, the natural, organic process by which the strongest survive . . . that's not happening. What we have instead is favor-trading, networking, and other sordid forms of insulation from the culling edge of the evolutionary razor. When the awards outnumber the candidates, we're heading for the Wall. With no brakes and the steering locked.

But . . . in this corner, Joe R. Lansdale. Son of a carnival fighter whose truest legacy was stand-up values. Married to a genuine, long-stemmed Texas blonde beauty he surely doesn't deserve on the basis of his looks. Blessed with two glorious children, with his own legacy to pass along. A high-ranking *karateka* whose body shows the marks of tuition. A man who has worked with his hands from everything to slopping hogs to self-defense—and who is still ready to go either one if pushed.

Here comes Joe R. Lansdale, now. Walking a samurai's walk. If you can't get down, you best step aside.

This is the real deal.

The true, blue haiku.

Reading Joe's work, I'm reminded of nothing so much as a fine pit bull. No posturing. No threat-displays. Ready to pay what it costs. Not the biggest . . . but sure he's the best. Dead game. And driven by love.

In real fights, styles don't matter. The champions all have that purity of line, that ability to step inside the other guy's rhythm. Focus. Laser-tipped concentration. Dedication.

Read Joe Lansdale and see it for yourself. *Feel* it. You can always tell when a virgin's writing a sex scene. You can spot the kinetic impossibility of the violence when the writer hasn't been in a fight. You'll never see this in Joe's work—it's not there. He knows "hard" isn't the same as "heartless." Read Joe Lansdale and see the true writer's gift . . . he's felt it, and he'll let you in on the feeling.

He's driven the cars, chased the diamonds, known the girls, listened to the psychopaths. Felt . . . and fought . . . the fears. He's been in the ring, been out of luck, been down . . . and come back. He knows you have to bring some to get some.

He knows the truth. He writes to share it.

It's called empathy, people. You use it, or you lose it. And it's a delicate line. In this repulsive age of Serial Killer Chic, Joe hands us *Drive-In Date* . . . understated ice. Anyone titillated by this horror classic needs to be on medication. Joe can do whatever he wants to do, from respectful homage to the Gold Medal paperback originals of the 50's like *Savage Season* and *Cold In July* to theme-anchored fantasy like *Cadillac Desert* to blood-morality tales like *Steel Valentine*. He can write about shape-shifting demons—he can write about swamp-dwelling humanoids. He can write comic books, movie scripts, hilarious film critiques. He can create his own genre . . . some miraculous fire-dance between private eye, horror, and comedy. You don't believe me, check out *The Events Concerning a Nude Fold-Out Found In A Harlequin Romance*. He can deal with the *consequences* of things . . . and their roots. Look at *The Night They Missed the Horror Show* or *By Bizarre Hands* and you'll see what I mean. Feel it, too.

Subtle doesn't mean secret. Joe is right out there with what he hates: domestic violence, racism, bullies, child abuse, sexual sadism . . . dishonorable creatures doing ugly things. He's not writing some nonsensical "noir" fiction . . . he's shining a white-hot light.

Act of Love is a raw book. A high-wire act by an then-emerging writer. A significant stage in Joe's evolution, going back for more than a decade. You can see the struggle for mastery. And the refusal to surrender. Is it his "best" work? I don't think so. With Joe Lansdale, naming anything his "best" is a judgment subject to rebuttal. Not just because reasonable people could disagree, especially given his huge body of work, but because Joe's *working* all the time. He may be swimming at the horizon of writing perfection . . . but he's not getting tired.

This is an important book. Proof that Joe understands survival. And never stops punching. Joe R. Lansdale is an American Original. We won't see his like again.

Remember I told you that the genre market was in trouble? A dragon's coming soon . . . coming down hard. It's going to walk through the jungle, clearing out the dead vines with its breath, stomping on those that can't get out of the way. A hard, cleansing wind is going to blow.

Joe knows this too. He's been getting ready a long time.

And when Darwin shows up, Joe's going to kick his ass.

Who knows what evil lurks in the hearts of men?
— From the opening of **The Shadow** *radio program*

Blood! Bah!
— Michael Le Faucheur

It will have blood
*— William Shakespeare (**Macbeth**)*

Viva la Muerte! (Long live death!)
— Millan Astray

I could not love except where death
Was mingling his with Beauty's breath . . .
  — *Edgar Allan Poe*

Oh let me love you
with this blade?
In passions lull
your tiny breast lines heave,
I watch them fade

For I shall dream
of falcon flight
and pray
for all consuming night
and I will be your minute man,
and show you love,
I know I can!

Oh let me love you
with my blade.
  — *Mignon Glass (**The Psycho's Song**)*

THE BEGINNING . . .

Pearl Harbor is not just the place the Japanese bombed; it has a namesake, so christened for the blood that's been shed there — more blood than the original Pearl Harbor ever saw. It's a vicinity in the Houston, Texas ghetto called The Fifth Ward. It's just off Lyons Avenue (Soul Street) and Jensen, and if you're thinking of suicide, or if you want to get cut from ear to ear, it's the place to stroll late at night, jingling your money. For that matter, you don't need money. Saying goes, "There's folks down there can't sleep at night unless they've killed somebody."

So death, blood and violence are no strangers to Pearl Harbor and The Fifth Ward ghetto. It's a tight, black world crowded with both flesh and poverty; a cesspool of despair. Over thirty-four percent of its residents live below the poverty level compared with Houston's ten percent. The median income of The Ward is just over five thousand dollars, while Houston's overall average is almost ten thousand dollars.

The people of this ghetto, like ghettoes everywhere, are swamped in the darkness of ignorance, pain and destruction. But for all its seething hatred and explosive violence, it is endowed with a peculiar sort of pride fostered by emptiness and desperation. A pride that allows its members to not only live in pain, but in occasional joy . . . and sometimes it must share in something that is not quite either. Something that is certainly no joy, and something beyond the pain of The Ward's daily existence.

Something akin to horror.

Something that did not end there, but began there.

Something like the arrival of the cold, calculating madman who would come to be known as "The Houston Hacker."

SUNDAY . . . 11:58 p.m.

Thinking back on the blood and her struggles, he had an erection.

He came out of the dark and into the weak glow of the street lamps; lamps long dirty and specked with the splattered ruin of kamikaze bugs. The ankle-length raincoat he had been wearing was now folded over the bloody bayonet and his freshly acquired treasure. The raincoat was tucked tightly beneath his arm. There was nothing hurried about his steps, but then his movements were not lazy either. There was black greasepaint on his face, gloves on his hands and a close-knit cap pulled tightly on his head.

He went to the brown Volkswagen parked at the curb. It had been stolen for two hours and thirty-five minutes. His own car he had left in an all-night parking lot. It was within walking distance of the Jack-In-The-Box where he had, with his ring of keys — the same sort used by professionals for repossessing automobiles — stolen the Volkswagen to use for tonight's job. The first job of many.

He unlocked the Volkswagen, slid inside and started the engine. While the motor idled he used the handkerchief to clean his face. There was a jar of cream he had brought with him to make the task easier that sat on the passenger's seat. From time to time he dipped the corner of the handkerchief into the cream and applied it to his face.

No way could he fool someone into thinking he was black, but at a distance, which was the only way he was going to be seen — little nigger bitch in the alley exceptioned, of course — it was an effective disguise. He had even worked on his walk so that it would appear black. He had once seen a movie called *Cotton Comes To Harlem*, and in that movie a black junkie had identified some masked and gloved men by the way they ran. He had said something like, "I know they was white, man. They ran white."

Well, he could walk black. He put the lid on the cream, folded the blackened handkerchief away in his blue-jean coat pocket, put the Volkswagen in gear and eased away from the curb, headed away from the heart of Houston's nefarious ghetto, The Fifth Ward.

The Fifth Ward. He thought of that, tasted the words on his lips. The Fifth Ward. The words were sweet. Fear defeated, he thought, destroyed like an ant beneath his heel. When he had been in high school all the boys used to say, "If you want to get your guts cut out, just cruise on out to Niggertown and ride up and down Jensen late at night, and one of them woolies will do it for you."

He smiled at the memory. It had been a fear of his childhood, and he had dreamed of defeating it. He was not a man to merely dream anymore — and there was more to it than defeating fear, much more. There was the enjoyment to be gained, enjoyment he had long denied himself, except in dreams, and except for an occasional dog or cat beneath his knife. But that was not enough, not anymore.

Mentally, while walking down the street, while at work, he watched people — especially women, mostly women — and thought how it would be to remove their arms and legs and heads, and how they would look. Little rag dolls pulled apart, liquid, red stuffing, flowing out and away, and he wondered too how it would be to drink their blood, to lap it from the floor with his tongue like a dog. The taste of it and the smell of it had haunted him in his dreams, but tonight, back in that cold, hard alley it hadn't been a dog or a cat, it had been a woman.

He thought again of his childhood fears of The Fifth Ward, said aloud to himself, "If there's going to be any goddamned gut cutting around here, I'll be the one to do it."

God, he almost pounded the steering wheel in delight. It had been wonderful! Much better than his dreams. Much, much, much better. The bayonet a shining arc in the dim street light. The blood, a crimson splatter of draining life, her agonized twistings, her muffled screams trying desperately to penetrate the fabric of her panties. And that had certainly been a good part, putting that razor sharp bayonet against her throat, forcing the panties into her mouth, telling her all the while that his intentions were rape, nothing more. Then when she was gagged, and her arms tied behind her back, he had pulled the blade in a slow arc across her belly, letting it slice deep into her ebony flesh, watching the blood bead like shiny, red pearls pulled up from the black depths.

And then the memory faded a bit.

He would have to work on that part, learn to concentrate and prolong the victim's agony and his pleasure, but he did remember the stench and the sound of her intestines pushing free of her abdomen, swelling out of her belly like coils of rope, and then he had taken her, right there in the alley on cold concrete amidst the smell of blood, intestines, excrement, garbage, urine and cheap wine.

Easy as eating cake. He had just slipped his penis out between the buttons of the raincoat and slammed it to her. Her face, even in dying, had been a beautiful sight. Twisted, disbelieving, the eyes losing their fire, falling away into the distance of her dead mind.

The dead eyes had been fascinating!

When he had finished, he had simply removed the raincoat, folded it inside-out over the bayonet and his little prize, and left the body to the night.

Delicious. It had been delicious, and best of all, the smell of death was still with him.

MONDAY . . . 12:02 a.m.

High on wine and ready to piss, looking for the darkness of a back alley to let it go, the black wino known only as Smokey found the first hacked body, and upon seeing it through wine-filmed eyes in the halflight of a bug-swarmed streetlamp, lost not only the wine in his stomach, but the remains of a sardine and cracker meal as well.

At first he thought (wanted to think) he was seeing a mannequin surrounded by garbage. Garbage was a common sight and smell in Smokey's world, and for that matter, so was blood and sudden death. He had narrowly escaped Old Man Death a few times himself. But this was something much worse than a Saturday night knifing or bottle beating. This was mutilation for the sheer joy of it — sickness, not frustration or anger. For the mannequin was no mannequin at all, but what was left of a local poke and hop head, Bella Louise. Even in her present state Smokey recognized her. Not more than an hour ago she had taken his fiver, dropped her pants, and with her hands on another alley wall — not even as well lighted as this one — had let him rut out his passion in a quick succession of bumps and groans.

What Smokey had thought to be strewn garbage was in fact intestines. They had been ripped from the body and tossed about. There was enough of the face left to be recognized. Her nostrils had been slit, her lips removed, and a slash as wide as a finger and twice the depth ran the length of her face, forehead to jaw. Her head was nearly disconnected from her body. It clung to her torso by a thick, bloody hunk of flesh and a whitish fragment of bone. One of her eyes was missing. Her once blue blouse was dark and wet and pulled up beneath her armpits. Her formerly pendulous breasts had been hacked away to leave dark, wet wells. Her belly was split from breast bone to crotch. The pants she had worn (Had they been glitter green? Smokey tried to remember), were nowhere to be seen. There was something white, specked with dark blood, stuffed in her mouth.

The smart thing, thought Smokey — and he would certainly think this later — would be to turn out of the alley and step like hell. Let The Fifth Ward take care of its own. It had in the past, it could in the future. But he couldn't. Bella had been little more to him than two minutes in the dark, but some second sense seemed to tell him that this wasn't any of The Ward's doing. No. This was something altogether different, and as much as he hated the goddamned hassling cops, he was going to patter on down to that wine store he robbed from time to time, find a phone and give The Man a bell.

MONDAY . . . 2:38 a.m.

Home: that greasy part of the city stuffed with stink and death. He could afford more. Much more. He had the money, but his apartment was enough. In fact, it was perfect. There was the smell of the street cluttered with garbage and the smell of the old, the sick and the dying. The apartment house was practically an old folks' home due to the cheap rent, mostly inhabited by the old, wrinkled women perpetually in flannel nightgowns and fuzzy shoes that looked like dead, dyed rabbits.

Sometimes he wanted to cut those old women.

Do the old bleed as well as the young? He wondered.

Sometimes, he could hardly sleep for wondering. Sometimes he wanted to take his bayonet and go downstairs and take the old woman on the bottom floor and do things to her, the things he had done to the girl in the alley.

But he was too smart for that. He lived by a motto: You don't piss in your own sink, you don't shit on your own rug. You play it cool, close to the chest. The city is full of fruit just there for the plucking. Ripe, young fruit and that which was aged as well.

Someday an old one though. Most certainly. One like his

27

mother. All sass and filthy mouth with wine breath and dark gums full of rotten teeth, eyes full of past sins . . . Yeah, like his old lady.

And when he found her . . . and he would find her . . . Hack! Hack! Hack!

He climbed the stairs with the raincoat tucked securely under his arm. He unlocked his apartment and went into darkness. He went to the dining table without bothering with the light. He knew his apartment well without lights, what little there was to know. The table, two chairs, a writing desk with typewriter and a foldout bed was the bulk of its contents. There was a little kitchenette and a small bathroom with both tub and shower. The floor was ancient wood, dirt-brown and peeling with the heads of nails staring up from the boards like small, flint-grey eyes.

He took off his gloves, laid them on the table. He unwrapped the raincoat on top of them, removed the bayonet from the mounds of flesh there, and put it on the table. He picked up the hacked breasts in both hands and squeezed them like sponges, felt the blood drip onto his fingers and run down his sleeves.

"Now, that's copping a feel," he said aloud.

He put the meat back on the raincoat, went over and turned on the light. His hands and the light switch were bloody. He would clean them later. He went back to the table, and cradling the hacked breasts in the raincoat, he took his treasure to the rust stained sink, set the package on the drainboard. He took a glass from the overhead cabinet, set it beside the raincoat, and then, carefully, he lifted the raincoat, and pinching one corner of the folded vinyl into a sort of funnel, he drained a quarter glass of blood from it. He drank the blood. It seemed like an elixir; cold, congealing, but still liquid. He got a knife out of the utensil drawer and set about slicing up the flesh for frying.

PART ONE:
THE HUNT BEGINS

It is the enemy whom we do not suspect who is most dangerous.

— *Rojas*

Crime is common. Logic rare. Therefore it is upon the logic rather than upon the crime that you should dwell.

— *Sherlock Holmes*

What song the Syrens sang, or what name Achilles assumed when he hid himself among women, although puzzling questions, are not beyond conjecture.

— *Sir Thomas Browne*

Clues are the traces of guilt that the criminal leaves behind.

— *Theodore Reik* (**Myth and Guilt**)

1

MONDAY . . . 4 a.m.

His name was Marvin Hanson.

He was black as the pit and ugly as an ape. He was a police lieutenant. Plainclothes. Homicide division. He had short arms and abnormally large hands with fingers as thick as frankfurters. He was five feet, ten inches tall, but due to the width of his shoulders, the thickness of his body, he didn't look a fraction over five feet, seven inches. His closest friends, all three of them, called him Gorilla. Everyone else called him Marvin, Mr. Hanson, or Sir. A few close associates called him simply Hanson. This was none of Hanson's doing. He was just the sort of person that demanded respect; begrudging respect perhaps, but respect, nonetheless.

Right now Hanson was in one of his least cheery moods. A two a.m. phone call had rung him out of Rachel's arms, out of his warm bed and out into the night. That, he supposed, was part of the price you paid for being a cop. Constant interruption, discomfort and aggravation. Not to mention ulcers, hemorrhoids and bunions.

In spite of his mood, as always, Hanson was an efficient cop, if a bit on the rough side. He was street-wise and back alley mean. He was also surprisingly well-educated, most of it self-acquired. This was a trait that often surprised people. From the looks of him, he seemed like the type to spend his life turning over the big rock and bursting dirt with a shovel.

Hanson had been brought up in The Fifth Ward, but as he was fond of telling his daughter, JoAnna, he had escaped and made of himself what he always wanted to be. A cop.

Sometimes he regretted that decision, regretted being a cop.

Tonight was one of those times. But it was a way of escape. A way out of The Ward, out of the slime and into the mainstream of life.

But maybe he hadn't managed to escape at all. Sure, he no longer lived in that filthy squalor, but his assignments were most often located there. He was from The Ward. He knew The Ward, and therefore, he was the right cop for The Ward. That didn't make him like it any better. He had their grudging respect, but on the other hand, he was still an Uptown, Uncle Tom, Nigger Cop to them. He thought it odd that the blacks complained about the ghetto, wanted out, but when one of their number made it out, he or she was immediately an Uncle Tom. Catch 22.

There were two other men in the hot, smoky room with

Hanson. One was his partner; a tall, rawboned, white man with orange-red hair, green eyes and a Howdy Doodie face. Not to mention poorer taste in grey suits than Hanson had. His name was Joe Clark. He had been a plainclothes detective for just over three years. Before that a city cop, and before that a criminology major. Hanson started off being suspicious of criminology majors, and with good reason. Most of them were about as helpful as a plugged revolver. They were good at technical things, like getting fingerprints off paper or analyzing hair and blood, but they couldn't read the truth or a lie in a man's face any better than they could read a blank wall. They all interrogated their prisoners just alike — or nearly all — and that was in a manner that said: Nothing personal, it's just my job. I know society has treated you rough and the world has shit in your face, but see, this is what I do for a living. I'm supposed to ask questions. Nothing personal.

Bullshit!

It was always personal. There were no two sides to this business. There were the good guys and the bad guys. Oh, sometimes you had to get down on their level, but the result was the black hats behind bars and the white hats triumphing. It was as simple as that.

Clark, criminology major or not, was an exception to the rule. He, like Hanson, took it personal. Being a cop was part of his fiber, the sinew of his soul. He wasn't afraid of death or dying. He wasn't afraid of going all the way. Not striving to nail a guilty party, not really caring if he got a confession out of a murderer or not, was like putting a bloody rabbit between a hound's jaws, turning your

37

back and saying ever so politely "Please don't eat the rabbit, Mr. Dog." It just didn't work.

Clark was a good partner. Both Hanson and Clark were deeply hurt by the wholesale corruption associated with the Houston Police Department. Hurt most because most of it had proven true. It was rampant and blatant. But he and Clark tried. They got rough occasionally; more often they threatened violence — not exactly legal, true, but very effective. The mere sight of Hanson's massive paws clenching and unclenching was enough to make a person feel very confessional.

The third man in the room, Smokey, was twisting his faded, blue baseball cap in his hands as if it were something alive he was trying to strangle. He was sitting in a hardback chair, slightly slumped forward, legs spread defensively. He looked up at Hanson with rheumy eyes; milky swirls crowding blue, a white man's eyes in a black man's face.

"I knowed I'd been better off to let that 'ho lay," Smokey said.

Hanson, standing, hovering over Smokey like The Sword of Damocles, said, "Nobody's hasslin' you. Start over."

"Man," Smokey whined, "I done told you."

A little less patient than before, Hanson said, "Start over. I've known your sorry ass all my life, Smokey. You ain't worth a damn and you know it, I know it, and anyone that's ever heard you run your mouth long as five minutes knows it. But I don't think you killed Bella. That take a load off your mind?"

"But I look good for it, don't I, Cap'n?"

"That's lieutenant, not captain. And no. You don't look good

38

for it. If you'd cut that gal like Higgins says she was cut, you'd have
. . . "

"You ain't seen her?" Smokey interrupted.

Hanson shook his head. "I was assigned to this case, instant
like. A phone call and Higgins says the Captain wants me on this
one. So I'm on it. That's all I know. Higgins said it was messy.
Okay, Smokey? All your questions answered? I'm supposed to ask
the questions here. Got me?"

Smokey nodded.

Hanson took a bulky King Edward from his coat pocket, fired
the cigar with a paper match and sucked smoke, blew it out his
nostrils lazily. "Like I said, it doesn't look like you did it, but. . . "
Hanson paused and made a production of puffing his cigar.

"But what?" Smokey asked dryly.

Hanson leaned down close to Smokey's face, smelled the
rotten teeth and stale wine breath. *"You could be made to look good
for it.* I mean if you don't give us all you know, and give it straight,
it could really start to look bad for you, Smokey. Real bad. Savvy?
Now let's run through this one more time, and you answer my
questions straight and don't try to con me, 'cause you ain't got the
good sense to con me . . . and don't think them rubber hose days
are completely behind us. You've heard what happens to folks that
want to get smart with us. Haven't you, Smokey?"

"Yeah, I heard."

Clark could just manage not to laugh. It was a cruel trick for
Hanson to play on the old man, but it was one that would garner
immediate results. Because, unfortunately, the Houston Police

Department had a reputation for following up threats.

"You understand what I'm saying?" Hanson asked Smokey.

"I get your drift."

"You're going to tell it straight?"

"I'm going to tell it straight, Mr. Hanson."

"That's nice. I thought you were," Hanson said standing upright, removing the King Edward from his mouth and holding it cupped in his huge, bear-like paw. "I never thought differently. Not for a minute. Not for a second." Hanson turned to Clark, said, "Turn on the tape recorder, Joe."

"Ready?" Clark asked Smokey. It was one of the three words he had said during the entire interrogation. The other two words had been, "Sit down."

Smokey nodded that he was ready. He gave the twisted ball cap a breather, put it on his knee and looked down at it like he had just discovered it perched there.

Clark turned the recorder on.

Hanson said, "State your name, please."

"Smokey."

"Your full name, please."

"Clarence Montgomery. My daddy gave me that name Smokey and that's what folks call me mostly."

"Tonight you claim to have found a body. A woman you knew named Bella Louise Robbins. Could you tell us where that occurred?"

"I don't claim nuthin'," Smokey said. "I did find Bella all cut up . . ."

"Could you tell us where?" Hanson interjected.

"Hell, Mr. Hanson, you know where."

To Clark, Hanson said: "Will you turn off the tape recorder, please."

Clark turned off the tape recorder.

Smokey fearfully stretched his thick lips over his rotten teeth, said, "I fucked up, didn't I?"

Hanson nodded his head slowly. "You fucked up. Just answer the questions when I ask them. Make it short and sweet like. Like you're telling somebody that hasn't ever heard it before. You got that?"

Smokey nodded.

"I said, have you got that?"

"I've got it."

"I don't want to have to cut off the recorder again and explain it over."

"No sir."

"If I have to cut off the recorder again, I send Joe out for the rubber hoses and a pair of wire pliers."

"Wire pliers. What for? What's the pliers for?"

"You don't want to know. Gonna do it right?"

Smokey nodded.

"What?"

"Yeah."

"Yeah what?"

"I'm gonna do it right."

"Turn it on, Joe."

Clark clicked the recorder into service again. Smokey gave his story, straight this time, brief and without interrupting the flow of the tape. When he was finished they let him go. They could have held him, but saw no reason to. Smokey had been little help, other than turning in the body in the first place, and Hanson admitted to Clark that that surprised him.

"Why do you think he turned it in?" Clark asked.

Hanson shook his head. "Don't really know, but I got this feeling."

"Alright, Sherlock. What's the feeling?" Joe shook out a Kool and lit it with a Bic lighter.

"It's just a feeling."

"Yeah."

"No evidence for it."

"Tell me. You and I have talked about cop feelings before. We put some stock in them, right?"

Hanson blew out some smoke. "Yeah right."

"Right now, tell me quick, gut reaction. Why did he do it? Why did he come in when normally he wouldn't have?"

Hanson put his hip into the long table that the tape recorder was perched on, puffed his cigar until his head was swarmed in grey smoke.

"I think he turned it in," Hanson said, "because he senses something. Something that you get from living on the street. You heard how he described the body. He was almost ill. I know for a fact that Smokey's seen quite a few stabbings and cuttings. Even done one or two minor surgeries himself. He was scared because it wasn't, in his mind, or mine either, for that matter, the work of a spontaneous killer."

"I'll agree with that," Joe said.

"It was premeditated and done for pleasure. Smokey said Bella looked like a butchered hog, only messy. It was deliberate mutilation, if his description was accurate."

"Lot of folks in The Ward are like that. Hell, Gorilla, you of all people know that."

"Mean, yes. I'll buy that. But this is something else. If Smokey's right, if it's as he says, I'm afraid we just might have something nasty on our hands."

"Something like a black Skidrow Slasher?"

"Maybe. Not many of you honkeys are going to cruise around The Ward after midnight, not unless you're selling a little white powder that some of the folks down there think they have to have to get up in the morning."

"Maybe it's a pusher that done it, disguised the killing to make it look like a nut murder. That's an angle. Bella could've been pushing drugs on the side, I mean her record shows that she's been picked up as a user before, nothing concrete in the eyes of the law, but you and I know. That's an angle, too. A pusher could have done it and covered his tracks. Or Bella could have been pushin' and someone decided they didn't need to pay for it, so they took it and did Bella in. Whataya think?"

"Maybe."

"But you don't think so, do you?"

"Not really."

"What do you think?"

"Don't know yet."

"Come on, Gorilla. What do you think?"

"I think it might be a good idea to start by seeing the body."

"Oh cheery," Clark said. "Let's go."

The morgue is open twenty-four hours a day.

There is always someone on duty. It doesn't close for holidays. Not Christmas, not good ole George Washington's birthday. It is the palace of death and examination. It is more constant than the city. It always has customers. They drop by at all hours of the night, most often arriving in white wagons with blue and red lights.

Tonight the morgue has a new customer. This customer is allowed special privileges. The head of the Houston Medical Examiner's Office is called from his sleep.

There has been a terrible death, they tell him, an unusual death, and tonight, as soon as possible, he must make a preliminary examination of the body, and tomorrow after he has rested (and don't sleep too long), he is to perform a detailed autopsy. The autopsy is not to find the cause of death, that is obvious, but to determine if the murderer has inadvertently left behind clues to his identity: blood not matching the type of the victim; skin beneath the victim's fingernails; pubic hairs; seminal fluid and the like. Not an overly complicated job. A job many at the morgue could perform. But in a case like this, a suspected "nut murder," the authorities want the best, and Doc Warren is the best.

Doc Warren arrives, slips into his work clothes: white smock over-lapped by green plastic bib-apron. With the assistance of a long, lean, similarly-dressed attendant, he rolls out the body for a look. The refrigerated air from the storage compartment spits its cold at the pair. They slide the body onto the rolling table with professional ease. The white sheet covering the body is stained with splotches of red. The pair hardly notice.

They wheel the body to one of the metal autopsy tables in the room that Warren affectionately calls "the slicing room," and even after all these years, Doc Warren once again bumps his head on the specimen scale that hangs at the head of the table, says his now classic line, "I'm gonna remember that one of these days."

The attendant makes with a dutiful smile.

The rolling table has a tilting device. They use it to shift the body to the autopsy table. Doc Warren reaches out and pulls back the sheet.

The attendant's eyes widen. He has seen much these last two years, but he has not seen the likes of this.

Doc Warren says flatly, "Ugly."

Without another word he begins his preliminary examination.

"Next stop, the morgue," Hanson says as they start for the downstairs mortuary; a place they had both been many times.

"All out for blood and guts," Clark announces. "Please try not to vomit on the floor and don't trip over a hacksaw."

But for all their exterior toughness and sandpaper approach

to police work, they were not looking forward to this little jaunt. Never did. But this trek was particularly distasteful. Smokey's words concerning Bella's appearance kept rotating in their minds. Like a butchered hog, he had said, only messy.

It would, of course, be easy to wait on the autopsy reports and read them, or talk to the man on the scene, Higgins, in great detail. But they would not wait. Words on paper did not drip blood. Words from the mouth of another officer, no matter how reliable, did not paint the same picture as the eye could deftly, and permanently, engrave on the brain.

Hanson had thought, and Clark had agreed, that if this was the sort of murder they suspected, they should see the results of the killer's work, the brutal art of his sharp bladed insanity. Not so much out of curiosity — there was, of course, that morbid element — but more to see what sort of lunatic they were up against, if in fact, it was a lunatic. Sometimes — more often than not — witnesses to a crime, or crime scene (even trained police officers) remembered the incident in a far more dramatic fashion than what they had actually seen. And often, eye witnesses who had seen the same thing would give drastically conflicting accounts.

Hanson, however, knowing Smokey for so many years, and knowing all that Smokey had seen and done in The Fifth Ward, doubted that in this case. Besides, there was nothing like a first hand view; nothing like a little senseless slaughter and mayhem to bring the cop blood to a boil and get it pumping so that when the trail got cold and the brain got fuzzy, they could always turn on the memory wheels and recall the slab scene, and maybe that alone could keep them going. Going until the killer was in the jaws of the law, weak-hinged as those jaws might be.

Hanson and Clark went downstairs to the morgue with faces set in stone, hearts on hold. For a little while, the humor stopped.

Old Doc Warren, white-haired, sallow-faced and ill-tempered, showed them the body: a mess of red whipped into black; a grotesque chocolate and cherry pudding of death. It barely resembled anything human, and it was worse — far worse — than either had suspected. Smokey had underplayed it. The pair, by later agreement, thought it the worst crime of the sort that either of them had seen, and Hanson had been on the force over twenty years.

Doc Warren, leading the pair with his stiff walk (Clark often joked to Hanson that Warren's vulture faced appearance and stiff walk were due to the fact that he was just one of the corpses that got bored down there and applied for a job), directed them to the lounge, and after the men were seated, he told them this about the corpse:

"It's unofficial, mind you, until I've made an autopsy, but from preliminary examination, I'd say the slash on her throat was the one that killed her. No Sherlock Holmes here. Nobody lives with their head dangling by a string — not unless they're the Frankenstein monster. I think he cut her throat and hacked on down to the bone in a frenzy."

"He killed her in anger?" Hanson asked.

"No. I mean frenzy. I mean it in the same way it's used to describe the feeding insanity of sharks and piranha. An uncontrollable urge, a temporary madness. In this case joy at the sight of blood and pain, or so I guess. The neck was hacked to pieces. You saw that."

"Don't remind me," Hanson said.

"Any of the other wounds were enough to do her in, the stomach for instance, but that would have taken longer. From the looks of the cuts on her hands and feet, and the nicks below her eyelids, I'd say he tortured her some. Removal of the lips, sexual organs, that's not uncommon in crimes like this."

"He did all that?" Hanson asked.

"You weren't looking very close," Warren said.

"I admit I didn't get down on my hands and knees and sniff."

Warren made a sour smile. "He stuffed those items into the ripped cavity of her stomach."

"Christ," Hanson said softly.

"He also knocked out a couple of her front teeth, probably when he was forcing her panties down her throat. The missing eye — which the investigating officer discovered in the alley — was probably dug out with the point of a sharp instrument. Most likely, considering the damage to the eye socket and the lid, something bigger than a knife. A sword or bayonet maybe. I think after killing her he was working on the body when this man — what's his name? — I have a terrible memory for those reports . . . "

Like hell you do, thought Hanson, but he said, "Smokey, or at least that's what's on your preliminary report from Higgins."

"Yes. Well, when this Smokey came up he had to leave her. Or maybe he just quit. Her arms were bound behind her back with her pants. That and the gag meant he planned to stay awhile."

"She raped?" Hanson asked.

"Can tell you later for sure. Probably. I can tell you this much. According to what the officer found after his search in the alley, and after reading his report and making my preliminary examination of the body, it's a certainty that the killer sliced off the breasts and took them with him."

"Sonofabitch," Clark said.

"And he just took his time," Hanson said. "Right there in the goddamned alley, easy as you please."

"People aren't exactly the investigative type down there," Doc Warren said. "Besides, that's part of the thrill for this guy. The fear of discovery. Sex offenders — and this *is* a sex crime, I'll stake my reputation on that — get off to that sort of thing. It heightens the act for them. It was probably that way with Jack the Ripper, The Zodiac Killer, The Boston Strangler and The Skid Row Slasher. All those crimes were committed right under people's noses. I think we've got a real screwo here. 'Course I'm not a psychiatrist, but I'd say he's a necrophiliac — a dead body lover; a dismemberer. That's why I say he wasn't finished with the body yet. I think he just got started with the head. The arms and legs were next.

"You know, Hitler was reputed to be a necrophiliac. I read once where a mutilated soldier's body excited him so much, they practically had to drag him off the battlefield."

"Yeah," Clark said. "I think I've heard that story, too."

"But this guy," Hanson said, "he's going to try and pull this sort of thing again, isn't he? He's going to make it a string. Right?"

"I'm no clairvoyant," Doc Warren said, "but from what I've seen in the past, and I've seen quite a bit in the many years I've been at this, and from what I've read and studied — and I admit to a certain morbid fascination with this sort of thing . . . "

"We always figured you were sort of . . . special . . . to want to do this sort of work in the first place," Clark said dryly.

Warren smiled, unoffended. "I'd say, my friends, just between us chickens, guessing you understand, this is probably just the beginning."

2

MONDAY . . . 7:02 a.m.

Dead tired, wishing at times like this that he lived closer to the precinct than the Pasadena suburb, Hanson drove home. He had moved to Pasadena some five years ago to get away from the hustle and bustle of Houston. He was shocked to discover how few blacks lived there. But the transition had been relatively easy once the neighbors discovered that he didn't hang huge, foam rubber dice from his rearview mirror and attach indiscriminate numbers of curb feelers to all his automobiles. For that matter, he didn't even like watermelon, peanut patties and RC Colas. He had been known to drop down on a box of Kentucky Fried Chicken, however, and there wasn't a black-eyed pea or a slice of white bread safe in the house. His growing paunch was testimony to that.

Sometimes it bothered him to think he might have moved into

the Pasadena neighborhood because it was "without color," as his old granddaddy had been fond of saying. He never thought of himself as being a radical. He wasn't ashamed of being black, but then again he wasn't proud of it either. He hadn't really had much say in the matter. What he was proud of was the fact that he had pulled himself up and out of that ghetto by his bootstraps, and his family would never know what it was to be hungry, cold and miserable. He knew what his relatives thought of him, most of them anyway. Behind his back they called him an Uncle Tom, a laundried nigger, a honkey lover and a white black man. The hell with them. Let them be black in the ghetto. He'd be black here in Pasadena in his cozy two-story brick house. It wasn't a fancy house. It wasn't really different than the others on the block, but it was his and the Savings and Loans'.

Tonight, however, these thoughts were merely fleeting diversions. The color scheme of Pasadena was the least of his worries. There was that nagging slab scene whirling around in the back of his brain. He hated it. He tried to cover it with other thoughts, but like a drowning victim, it eventually surfaced. *Christ! She hadn't even looked like something human.*

He tried to think of other things. Anything. He thought of home. Considered what he would do when he got there. He was tired but too keyed up to sleep. Perhaps he would eat a bite and read, and maybe, just maybe, he'd wake Rachel and see if he could find a bit of warmth there. But no, on second thought that wouldn't be such a good idea. First he had come in late last night from work and she had awakened. She always had been a light sleeper. And then there was the phone call this morning that put him on this crazy murder. No, a third awakening would not put Rachel in an amorous mood. He would stay buddies longer, and have a better sex life overall, if he let her have that extra hour of sleep before she prepared for work and driving JoAnna to school.

But at least she was there. Just knowing she was there was enough. It made his whole miserable job worthwhile.

It had to be worse for Joe. Living alone, divorced from Peggy after only a year of marriage. Nothing for him to do but go home to darkness and walls. After the divorce Joe had moved, and not once had Hanson been to visit. He didn't even know where Joe lived anymore. He had left Peggy the house and rented an apartment, but he never said where. They were partners and friends, but when their shift was done they went their separate ways and lived their separate lives.

But Joe was lonely. Hanson knew that. You don't have a man for a partner three years straight, a man you see more often that your wife, (perhaps part of the reason Joe was no longer married; perhaps part of the reason so many cops were no longer married) and not know something about him, not sense changes in his behaviour and see the sadness in his eyes.

Those thoughts gave way again to Bella. *Cut, ripped, mauled. The victim of a modern day werewolf.*

Hanson parked his blue, '75 Chrysler at the curb. The drive was full of Rachel's Buick and the old '55 yellow Chevy that he was going to fix and paint one of these days. Yeah. One of these days.

He sniffed the early morning air as he stepped from the Chrysler. Nothing like a lungful of pollution to start your morning. Pasadena, Texas wasn't nicknamed Stinkadena for nothing. In an odd way, this morning reminded him of mornings in The Ward. The odor was different, industrial puke instead of garbage, wine, sweat and urine, but it was still sickening. It made him long for those summer mornings on his granddaddy's farm. That had been paradise.

Crystal clear air, long drives from the farm into Tyler, Texas to buy supplies and what his granddaddy called staples: flour, sugar and salt. And then back to the fresh, tart smells of vegetable rows and new mown hay.

He had inherited that farm after his granddaddy had passed. But by then he was a grown man living in Houston and working for the police department. Last time he had seen the farm the house and barns were grey and stripping with the work of the weather. The fields were tall with weeds and grass. His brother, who had inherited nothing except black skin, tried to get him to sell it. But he would never sell. Never. Someday he would go back there, and someday that farm would smell of animals and vegetables again.

Someday.

Christ! Hanson thought. It's awful damn early in the morning to be philosophical. As he closed the Chrysler door night was fading at the edges, giving over to the day. That was supposed to symbolize something. The turning of confusion into order. The rebirth of the Phoenix.

Fat chance! Not in Houston, Texas. There would never be a new dawn for that world of concrete, steel, pollution and crowded human flesh. Each day was another wallow in the slush. More death and destruction, and one more job for one more cop.

Day one every morning.

Day one forever.

It was like being a janitor. You could come in on schedule, sweep and mop, wax and throw out the garbage. But next day it was right back again, sometimes worse than the day before. You never made real progress. You just kept it where folks could walk for a few hours without getting bubblegum on their shoes. It was the same way with a cop. Temporary order, nothing more — and that, precarious order at best.

Poor Bella. A street whore swept out with the rest of the slush.

The house was dark.

Upstairs Rachel would be sleeping, soft-brown and snug in the blankets. In less than a half-hour she would be up and at it. Dragging JoAnna out of bed and getting her off to school and herself off to work.

Next year JoAnna had college. What a nag. Money, money, money. More money than a cop with a mortgage and too many bills could afford. But he'd manage somehow. He and Rachel always did. That was his motto: "We'll manage."

He unlocked the door and slipped inside, went to the kitchen, turned on the light and went to the refrigerator. He opened the door and felt the cold, frosty breath of the machine.

. . . Cold. That's what preserved bodies. Bodies like Bella's . . .

He got a glass down and poured himself a glass of milk. It was tasteless. He couldn't get Bella off his mind. A woman he didn't even know. A cheap streetwalker with about as much class as bubblegum jewelry. But there was no way he could push it out of his brain. Not with the worries of others; not with worries and thoughts of his own. She was there as if she had been burned in with a branding iron.

What a fucked up job. All hours of the day or night he was on call. Eat fast, sleep light and keep running. Never a break. Never a moment's peace. Run, run, run, and visit with the dead.

Hanson took a green plastic bowl of tuna mix from the refrigerator and a loaf of bread from the shelf. He took a fork from the utensil drawer and spread tuna on bread, poured himself another glass of milk. He sat at the kitchen table and ate, not tasting the food or the milk. When he was finished he put the bowl in the sink and ran water into it. That was something he tried never to forget, because if he did, boy did Rachel give him hell.

"Makes the washing easier," she'd say.

Next Christmas he was going to get her a dishwasher. No more hot suds for his baby.

He filled the glass with water and set it in the sink next to the bowl. He put the fork in the glass and put the milk and bread away. Wished too late that he had put a slice of cheese on his sandwich. He turned off the kitchen light, went into the livingroom and flipped on the light. The room was paneled in red mahogany — what room there was to see. Most of the walls were hidden by rows of bookshelves. He may have grown up poor, he may have lived in the ghetto, but his granddaddy had taught him to read and to love books. As a child he had owned one prized possession: A library card. It was hell for him to get to the library, but when he made it he always checked out his limit. In the summers he practically lived there behind one of those long, wooden tables; a world tucked firmly between his fingers; a world made up of paper, ink and imagination.

His brother Evan couldn't even read and write his name. He had become a boxer. He wasn't very successful at his trade. He wasn't bad, but he wasn't great either, just second-rate. I should have been the boxer, Hanson thought. I've got the hands for it, the chin and the heart. That was all his brother had had — heart. A heart like a stallion.

In a back alley not far from where Bella had been found, a teenager full of smack put a switchblade knife in that stallion-like heart for three dollars and forty-seven cents. And that was all for Bubba "The Kid" Hanson. Just another cold, dead nigger with a blade in his pump.

Death. It was certainly on his mind tonight. It was as if suddenly the bowl of his head had filled up with all the death it could stand and was overrunning like a clogged toilet. Twenty years on the force, and tonight, he felt as if he were coming to the end of his rope.

Maybe it was all the years of thinking of yourself as one of the good guys, arresting scum and seeing them on the street the next day due to some hotshot lawyer with all the scruples of a Gestapo agent. Yeah, maybe that was it, and maybe he should say the hell with it all.

At least for the moment that was exactly what he was going to do. The hell with it.

Hanson walked about the room, ran his fingers along the spines of the books. What did he want to read? He needed something to distract him; something to suck up his self-pity; something to rest him. Tired or not, he was too geared up for sleep. He touched Chandler's *The Big Sleep*. Nope. Too real for tonight. His fingers caressed *The Glory of the Hummingbird* by De Vries. Yep that was it. Light, fast and well written. He chose the leather chair next to the window, parted the curtains a bit before sitting down, and then holding the book up to the glowing light, he began to read. He read until the words rode each other piggy back and the book dropped from his big, limp hand.

And he dreamed.

In the dream Bella, cut and bloody, her head dangling by a strand of ragged flesh, rose from the slab in the morgue and walked. Zombie-like she walked, every step puddling pools of cold, inky blood. Her hands were no longer bound behind her back by her green, sequined pants. Her arms hung loosely at her sides. Her ripped torso dripped entrails. Intestines hung so low that she nearly stepped on them. Slowly she raised one bloody hand and pointed a finger at Hanson. He could not see himself in the dream, but he knew the finger was pointed at him. Her lipless mouth opened, moved, but no sound came out. She came closer. Her mouth was still moving. Blood leaked at the corners but still no sound. She reached out with her red streaked hand to touch Hanson.

"Wha . . . !"

Hanson came awake, Rachel's hand resting on his shoulder.

"Marve," she said. "You okay?"

"Huh . . ." Light streamed through the window, lay across his body in yellow slats. *The Glory of the Hummingbird* lay in his lap. Rachel, smooth as silk, the color of creamed coffee, smiled the smile.

"You were having a nightmare," she said, sitting down on the arm of the chair. She was wearing a plaid, ankle-length robe. It wasn't the sort of outfit that would look good on most women, but Rachel wasn't like most women. Hanson could smell her just-out-of-the-shower, fresh-soaped scent. She picked up the book. "De Vries gave you a nightmare?"

"No. Not De Vries."

Rachel's dark, brown eyes became serious. "What then?"

Hanson smiled, reached up to touch her thick afro hairdo. On the sides and the back it was almost to her shoulders.

"You have very nice hair," Hanson said.

"The nightmare, Marve. What was it about?"

"Work."

"About work?"

"Work brought it on."

"Tell me about it."

"Nothing to tell really . . . Little something just got to me, that's all."

"What got to you? You never have nightmares. I only remember you having one nightmare ever, and that was too many tacos that caused that."

"I still wince at the thought."

"About last night."

"There was a murder."

"I don't mean to sound cold, but in your business, isn't there always?"

"Yeah. But this one was different. Pressure is getting to me, I guess. It'll pass. Just too much blood this time."

"You need a vacation."

"Yeah. Maybe it's just an accumulation of years and bodies. No big thing."

"You still haven't told me about it."

"Honey, it's nothing . . . I mean it's nothing you want to hear."

"If it's bothering you let me hear it. Talking it out might help."

Hanson put his arm around her waist, pulled her off the chair arm and into his lap. He ran his fingers through her hair, wondering as he often did, what a beautiful woman like Rachel saw in a gorilla like him. He took the book from her hand and dropped it on the carpet. He said, "Kiss me, you fool."

Smiling she did, but briefly. "You going to tell me about it?" she asked, pulling away.

"Nope."

"Why not?"

"You always wake up beautiful."

Rachel grinned. "Baby, I stay beautiful."

"That's, 'I stays beautiful, baby.' You're falling down on your black accent."

"Weren't we talking about dreams?"

"Were we?"

"Don't change the subject."

"Subject?"

"Marvel!"

"Forget it, Rachel. It was a stupid nightmare. What time is it, by the way?"

"You're changing the subject again." Rachel looked at her watch, practically sprang out of Hanson's lap. "Shit! What am I doing sitting here. I've got to get JoAnna off to school and my ass off to work."

"Uh huh."

"You win this time," Rachel said feigning anger, "but next time . . ."

"Sure. Scoot, you'll be late."

And she went; graceful, quick and sensuous . . . and unfortunately, thought Hanson, off to work.

When Rachel was out of sight, Hanson picked up the De Vries book and returned it to the bookshelf. He stood looking at the other titles. One caught his eye: *Living the Good Life* by Helen and Scott Nearing. He hadn't read that one in years. When he had the farming bug the book had attracted him. They had a lot to say about homesteading, its joys and benefits. They were a bit eccentric, but there was good material there, a lot to be said for their simple existence. That reminded Hanson of his granddaddy's farm. Weedy, lifeless, weathered.

He took *Living the Good Life* down and opened it to the fly page.

"Daddy?"

Hanson turned to look at his daughter, JoAnna. His mind must really be preoccupied. It was rare someone could walk up on him that easy. Hanson smiled, "Good morning, sweetheart."

JoAnna had the same smile as her mother. In fact, except for the reddish tint to her afro hairdo, she was nearly the spitting image of Rachel. She was dressed in green slacks — a bit too tight, Hanson thought — and a white blouse that wasn't exactly lowcut, but a bit too revealing. The mounds of her breasts pushed at the fabric precariously. High school certainly had changed since he was a kid.

"Daddy, I need ten dollars."

"That's quite a good morning."

"Sorry. Mom said for me to ask and to hurry. I've got to finish getting dressed. I need it for cap and gown reserve."

"Ummm." Hanson returned the book to the shelf, took out his wallet and gave JoAnna two fives. "Graduation, huh?"

"Right." JoAnna slid the money into her pants pocket.

"You know, young lady, if you had a quarter in your pocket you could tell if it was heads or tails."

"What?"

"The pants. They're too tight."

"Oh, Daddy. They're not any tighter than anyone else's. I got to run and finish dressing. I haven't even got my shoes on." With that she turned and made for the stairs.

Graduation, Hanson thought. Christ, time slipped up on you . . . *suddenly he was sweating.*

Fear moved inside his brain like a lizard on a hot rock, and for a moment there was an image, fleeting, but identifiable. It was JoAnna, his lovely JoAnna, and she was as Bella. Ripped, ruined, wasted. Black whipped with red. A hunk of hamburger on a cold slab smoking with cold refrigerated breath.

He said weakly, "JoAnna."

JoAnna had just reached the stairs. "Wha . . . " And then she saw his face. She went to him quickly, took hold of his arm. "Daddy?"

"It's okay. Really."

"Daddy, are you all right?"

"Yeah."

"You sure?"

"Just dizzy for a moment."

"You're sweating."

"Just a little dizzy. Tired I guess. A cold maybe."

"You look like death warmed over. You better sit down." She held his arm as she guided him to the leather chair next to the window. Hanson sat. "You gonna be alright? You want me to get Momma?"

"No. I'm over it already. Just working too hard."

"You always work too hard. That's not news. Maybe you need to see a doctor."

Hanson smiled. "I'm alright, baby, really. Go on. Get ready for school, and don't say anything to Momma. It's passed. Really."

JoAnna worked her lip. He did look better. "You're all right, then?"

Hanson nodded.

"For sure? You're not just telling me that?"

"I'm not just telling you that. I'm fine. Nothing rest won't cure. I'm going to take a little nap when you two get out of my way. Okay?"

"Okay."

"Run along. I'll take a couple of aspirins in a minute."

"Alright," and she went.

Upstairs JoAnna added perfume and a few rake strokes to her hair, slipped on some soft, low cut shoes. She never could figure how Mary and the rest of the girls wore those big, clunky shoes to school. Her feet would have been so much mud by the end of the day. Dressing for the boys, she guessed.

Well, she did a bit of that herself. Actually for one boy, Tommy Rae Evans. They had been dating for over a month now, and each date had been a little hotter and heavier than the last. He had almost gotten into her pants last time, but at the last moment she had chickened out. If her daddy found out, well, as the old saying went, it would be too wet to plow.

Of course, if Tommy tried again this weekend — she smiled, and he'd be a darn fool not to — she just might let him.

"JoAnna," Rachel said as she stepped inside her daughter's room. "Ready yet?"

"Ready, Momma." JoAnna stood up from the dresser after a last look at her hair.

Rachel wrinkled her nose. "You've got too much perfume on, young lady."

"Just a drop or two."

"Big drops."

"I'll wash some of it off."

"Never mind. Come on, let's hustle."

"Momma?"

"What?"

"Daddy's acting kind of funny."

"He had a nightmare."

"Daddy? I've never known anything to scare him."

"A nightmare's different."

"I never even knew he had them."

"This is the second as far as I know. Once he dreamed a giant taco was chasing him."

JoAnna laughed. "Oh yeah, I remember that. I was just a kid then."

"Was?" Rachel said, raising her eyebrows.

JoAnna frowned. "All right. I was a smaller kid then."

"Come on, bigger kid." Rachel looked at her watch. "Oh hell.

8:30. I've got fifteen minutes to get you to school and then fifteen more to get to work. Come on."

They hurried down stairs, kissed Hanson goodbye and left. Both mother and daughter decided that he looked a lot better than when they had talked to him earlier. Neither thought anything more of it.

JoAnna was on time at school. Rachel was five minutes late for work.

When the women were gone Hanson fixed himself a cup of hot chocolate. He thought it might steady his nerves and help his sleep. He didn't understand what was happening to him. It was almost as if he had discovered another person inside his body. A person that feared and worried deeply. He had never been one to dwell on such things. He was always forging ahead, no matter what. Hanson the Juggernaut.

But that had been before Bella's murder. Why was this one getting to him? Did he, like Smokey, have a sort of inbred sense, warning him of worse things to follow?

And that brief vision of JoAnna. Had that been brought on by lack of rest . . . or had he for a fleeting moment actually peered into the future like a clairvoyant?

The hot chocolate tasted as bitter as lye. He poured it down the drain, went about the ritual of running water in the cup.

He wouldn't let dreams worry him. They were intangible and could not be grasped with the hands. Bella's murderer was quite a different matter. He could be grabbed and held. It was just a matter of time — and possibly deaths.

What was he worrying about?

A silly dream?

A bad flash concerning JoAnna?

It was all malarky. About the worst thing that had ever happened in their family was a missing dog. Nothing tragic within the immediate nucleus of his family unit had ever occurred. Nothing. Nothing at all.

3

MONDAY THROUGH FRIDAY

Monday, after Rachel and JoAnna had left and the hot chocolate had relaxed him somewhat, Hanson rested. He dozed off and on until shortly after noon. At that time he awoke, showered, drank coffee and had another tuna sandwich. He felt better, if not completely refreshed. He went about his obligatory duty with the water and the dishes, then called his partner, Joe Clark.

Clark answered on the third ring. Hanson offered to pick up Clark, adding that he would need the address however, as he had never even seen Clark's apartment. Instead, Clark offered to pick up Hanson. He said he had been sleeping when Hanson called, and that the drive from his place to Hanson's would do him good, let him shake some of the cobwebs out of his head.

Hanson agreed to this, and shortly after 1:30 p.m., Clark's arrival interrupted his reading of *Living the Good Life*. They drove to The Fifth Ward to begin their investigation; started at the scene of the crime.

Although this was the proper method, Hanson was a bit perturbed that he had been put on the case after the initial investigation had already occurred. It seemed foolish to him for the Chief to assign him to the case merely because he knew The Ward, and remove Higgins who also had Ward experience. He shrugged it off with his usual resignation that the upper ranks move in strange and mysterious ways.

The site of the murder was still marked off and restricted to authorized personnel only. Normally the crime scene would have already been abandoned, but in an unusual case like this, and considering the officer in charge had yet to investigate, bluesuits had kept vigil over the spot in shifts.

Hanson and Clark talked briefly with the cops in charge and began looking the site over. The investigation of a crime scene is important. The investigator must take into account that the scene is constantly changing, like the sands of a beach, shifting, moving. A good preliminary survey is the most important part of an investigation; one must observe and report accurately. In this case, however, Hanson had the equivalent to sloppy seconds. It irritated him a bit to know that what he and Clark were doing was merely formality and he told Clark as much. But he knew Higgins was a good investigator, and that he could depend on his report and on the crime scene photos.

Hanson told the bluesuits they could wrap the site up, they were through with it.

Next on the agenda was talking to people in The Ward, never a pleasant or welcome task on either side. Oddly enough, the residents were willing to talk, but none knew anything of importance. Hanson and Clark were surprised at this cooperation, and it further confirmed Hanson's suspicions that people living at street level had a higher developed sense of awareness — at least in matters like this. Somehow they knew there was more to this death than anger. Behind it was something quite different. Hanson sensed this too, and furthermore, he had Doc Warren's experienced opinion to back it up. He hoped his theory about The Ward residents and their heightened awareness, and Doc Warren's remarks, were off base — but that hope wasn't one he entertained seriously.

Much to the pair's dismay, they discovered that Philip Barlowe, reporter for *The Houston Bugle* had been there ahead of them. If any reporter would be on top of things it would be Barlowe, and worse yet, he had the uncanny knack of getting people to cooperate.

Barlowe was noted for his sensationalist reporting and his unjournalistic style. *The Bugle* was an odd cross between newspaper and scandalous tabloid; it was more than willing to print Barlowe's "ravings," as Hanson called them, and in fact, allowed him a personal column titled "Crime Scene: Houston."

Less than a year ago *The Bugle* had been a faltering newcomer, no competition for the well established *Houston Chronicle* or *The*

Houston Post, but by combining news with gossip, it had moved from a weekly joke to a daily profit; a publication to be reckoned with; a soldier of equal rank marching in a hard line with the more established publications. And perhaps, at least at times, stepping a step head in sales and popularity. Hanson considered it the pinnacle of muckraking, and therefore stuck staunchly to his beloved *Post*.

It was with a feeling of hopelessness that Hanson suggested they check in at the station. Both men knew the hard truth concerning this investigation. If proof of guilt, or apprehension of suspect, did not occur in the first forty-eight hours after the crime, chances were nothing would ever come of it.

Unless the killer struck again. And unless, this time, evidence of an incriminating nature was left behind.

This in mind, Clark drove them to the station.

Hanson and Clark shared a desk in the squad room. Since Hanson was of higher rank, he got to sit behind the desk. Joe was allowed a hardbacked chair next to it and a desk drawer of his own. He shared the other drawers with Hanson. Clark and Hanson often laughed about the situation. The desk, or "the office" as they called it, was of little importance anyway. They were seldom at the desk more than a few hours.

Together they pored over Higgins' report, read the autopsy report and looked at the photographs of the scene and the victim. The photographs brought Hanson's dream to mind, but he pushed it aside and got on with business. He made out a chart, something to help assimilate the facts and evidence. He went over them with Clark.

They were:

FACT: 1. Bella Louise Robbins is dead, murdered in an alley in a section of The Fifth Ward called Pearl Harbor.
2. Murder involved mutilation of the body, and it was confirmed by the autopsy report that she had been raped.
3. No suspects.
4. No witnesses to the crime. (Least none known, unless you want to count the killer, and I don't.)
5. Body discovered shortly after murder and reported. Discoverer has no real alibi, but not suspected.

Hanson handed his scrawl to Clark, said, "Can you add to that?"

Clark read it. "Nope, let's add the evidence." Clark took his pen and wrote:

EVIDENCE: 1. The body, autopsy reports confirming manner of death and rape.

He sat for a moment. "You know, Gorilla, this list shit is for the birds."

Hanson pulled the list away from him. "So's our evidence. Besides what you got here, we got zilch. And a chimpanzee could have told us this."

Hanson wrote on the list again, began a heading titled:

SPECULATION: A nut murder, probably the first of
many, as many as the sonofabitch can
get away with.

Hanson looked the list over for a moment, wadded it up and tossed it in the trashcan. "Well," he said, "the list always seems to work on television."

"Yeah, they've read the script before they make it out."

Hanson grunted.

Clark said, "I'll check with Evidence, right back."

Hanson was using his two-finger, hunt-and-peck method of typing a long overdue report when Clark returned with a newspaper under his arm and two sheets of paper in his hand. He didn't bother Hanson who was deeply considering the mystical complexity of the typewriter keys. Clark sat down, placed the two sheets of paper behind the typewriter and unfolded the newspaper. He took his ball point pen from his shirt pocket and began underlining something in the paper. When he was finished, he returned the pen to his pocket, put the paper in his lap, shook out a Kool and lit it, listened patiently to Hanson's . . . tap . . . tap . . . taptap . . . tap . . . tap . . .taptap.

Finally Hanson stopped, smiled. "You know, Joe. It's the black folks that are supposed to be cool. Here I am waiting you out, and you're not biting."

Clark said, "What?"

Hanson smiled. "What have you got, the suspense is killing me."

"Nothing, just a little something that's going to make you mad."

"So give it to me."

"First," Clark picked up the two sheets of paper behind the typewriter, "for formality's sake, here's the latest from Evidence. They didn't even find a hair that would help us. All the blood was the girl's. There wasn't any flesh under Bella's fingernails. He got her to cooperate, and got her hands bound too quickly, I guess. But what's going to piss you off is *The Bugle*."

"*The Bugle* always pisses me off."

"More than usual today."

Clark picked it from his lap, unfolded it and handed the newspaper to Hanson.

"Those places I've got marked," Clark said. "Read those."

Hanson read:

> Houston's annals of violent crime have once again opened to include a new and brutal murder. As special crime reporter for *The Bugle*, I have inside sources with the police . . .

Hanson looked up. "Inside sources with the cops. Who, I wonder? Who'd help this muckraking bastard?"

"Told you you'd love it."

"Christ, a cop spilling stuff like that."

"It probably doesn't matter."

"Yeah, except for the panic. All we need is everybody hopping because they think Houston's got its own Jack the Ripper."

"Doesn't it?"

"Maybe," Hanson said quietly. "But a cop . . ."

"You know better, Gorilla. It's not like all the cops in this precinct are honest. Haven't you been reading *Texas Monthly* and the newspapers lately?"

"So I like a few illusions. Most of these guys are good cops."

"The key word there, my friend, is most. It doesn't take more than one turd in the toilet to stink the place up."

"Very folksy."

"Thank you. Read on."

. . . and have the added benefit of seeing the autopsy reports, as well as having discussed this case with reliable sources. From my examination of the facts, it is this reporter's conclusion that this is merely the first of a chain of savage murders performed by another Jack the Ripper type . . .

Hanson raised his head here to say, "Oh, Christ."

"You must be at the Jack the Ripper part," Clark said.

Hanson didn't reply, just turned back to the column.

. . . or to be more exact, considering the condition of the body, A Houston Hacker. This killer shows no anatomical skill, but instead displays a desire to hack the body into ribbons of bloody flesh.

The article then went on to describe the condition of Bella's body in very unnewspaper-like terms. Hanson raised his head again.

Hanson said, "I can't believe a newspaper can get away with this." Then after a pause, "Had to be a cop tell him all this, it's too correct in detail."

"I'm afraid so," Clark said.

Hanson read more.

> Experts normally regard these types of murders as the work of a woman-hater or a paranoid schizophrenic, or both. This theory also suggests a man, although a woman is not necessarily ruled out . . .

Hanson stopped reading, tossed the newspaper to Clark.

"Crap!" Hanson said. "Pure crap! That's all we need. A lot of publicity and this guy will eat it up. Why does a newspaper editor allow this sort of shit?"

"Bread and circuses, Gorilla. Barlowe's been with *The Bugle* three years, and he's been writing that column a year-and-a-half. It's brought *The Bugle* up from a third-rate paper to a first-rate one."

"You call that first-rate?"

"It sells copies. They let Barlowe ramble a bit, get away from strict journalistic procedures, allow him to make a conjecture here and there, and the public eats it up. Blame them."

"This guy can't even write."

"He knows how to catch your eye."

Hanson leaned back in his chair, said stiffly, "Yeah, I guess he does at that. But that kind of stuff is going to set off every nut in the woodwork."

"They're nuts to begin with. Written words don't make people nuts."

"But it might set them off."

"If they're already cracked, anything might set them off. If we're going to censor violence, why not censor humor. Maybe that sets some of them off."

"That's ridiculous."

"Is it? If they're already cracked, anything could set them off. Like that guy down in San Antonio that cracked because a parade was going by his house. That was hardly violence that pushed him over the edge. We've got to quit coddling these goons. Fry em, hang em, but fuck temporary insanity, and I-did-it-because-I've-seen-too-many-Kojak-re-runs."

"Hell, Gorilla, you love crime stories, read the hell out of them. Did it make you crazy?"

"No . . . I mean I don't think so."

"Of course not. That's a bunch of lawyer malarky."

"Oh hell, drop it. We just might be lucky and this is the one and only murder by this beast."

"Yeah, and I just might find a thousand dollars stuck to my shoe when I get home."

"Maybe it was just some guy passing through. Maybe he's out of the state by now."

"Maybe."

"It's a thought."

"A weak one."

Hanson sighed. "You know, Joe, for a college trained cop, you sound pretty goddamned hardcore. Aren't I supposed to be playing your role?"

"I think maybe you are," Clark said, smiling. "But you see, I had a good teacher. A big, ugly nigger cop that looks like a fuckin' Gorilla."

Hanson laughed. "You asshole honkey."

Tuesday morning a note addressed to Philip Barlowe arrived at *The Houston Bugle*. It was in a plain blue envelope. Barlowe opened it. It was from the murderer, who now, following Barlowe's lead from the Monday column, referred to himself as The Houston Hacker. The note was turned over to police immediately. Although the police asked that *The Bugle* refrain from comment, Wednesday's *Bugle* ran Barlowe's column on the front page as a major news item.

The column read:

I never wanted to say I told you so, not to something as brutal and heinous as the recent Fifth Ward slaying of Bella Louise Robbins, but Tuesday morning a letter arrived here at *The Bugle* addressed to me. It was constructed of letters cut from magazines and newspapers, and although the police have asked that this information be withheld, we at *The Bugle* believe it is the right of our readers to be in the know. The contents of the note follows:

"You're right, Barlowe. It was me down in nigger-town the other night hacking up the little brown Jig. Little Brown Jig how I loved thee. And man did I have a ball, and in more ways than one.

Going to be at it again real soon, but I'm no nut, just a fun loving guy who likes to get his kicks, or maybe I should say hacks.

And by the way. That little nigger bitch had some tasty blood and I fried the tits, chicken fried. If you want, I'll send you the recipe.

Until then, *Let There Be Blood!*

THE HOUSTON HACKER

Chilling. The envelope and note have been turned over to authorities for examination. Let's hope our murderer is apprehended before he can kill again. But how do you catch a cold-blooded, calculating killer? Is the note authentic, or some sick joke? Personally, I feel it is the genuine article, and I think The Hacker will strike again. Soon. Remember, you read it first in *The Bugle's Crime Scene.* The most graphic and honest column concerning crime in the nation. Is the note authentic, or some sick joke? Personally, I feel it is the genuine article, and I think The Hacker will strike again. Soon. Remember, you read it first in *The Bugle's Crime Scene.* The most graphic and honest column concerning crime in the nation.

Joe Clark read the column, cut it out and put it in the lefthand drawer of the desk he shared with Hanson. Henceforth, he would collect all material having to do with The Hacker.

Hanson found the column so offensive he wouldn't even read

it. They had spent most of Wednesday in The Ward again, running down futile leads, and if there was one thing Hanson didn't need, it was to top off another "perfect" day with *The Bugle*.

Thursday a brown Volkswagen reported stolen Sunday night was found. It belonged to a James McBain. McBain worked as a cook in an all-night Jack-In-The-Box hamburger joint. He had not missed the car until Sunday midnight when his shift ended. He reported its disappearance Monday morning at 12:09. The Volkswagen was located in a nearby hospital parking lot. It was only six blocks away from the Jack-In-The-Box where McBain worked. There were stains on the seat. Lab technicians determined that they were of two origins:

(1) Black grease paint of the sort used by commandos to camouflage their faces at night.

(2) Blood which matched up with that of the victim Bella Louise Robbins.

Since McBain had an air-tight alibi — his job — he was subjected to simple questioning and released with his car.

Friday morning a blue envelope arrived at police headquarters in the mail. There was no return address. The mailing address was made up of letters cut from magazines and pasted to the envelope. The dispatcher, who was also responsible for the mail, was curious, and called Hanson to his desk.

After seeing the envelope, Hanson returned to his desk and slipped on a pair of surgical gloves he kept for handling evidence. He then opened the envelope and fished the letter out.

Suspicions were correct. It was from The Hacker.

It read:

Don't feel slighted, fuzz. Here's your own personal note. I'll have you some serious work soon. And don't just look for me in niggertown. I get around. He's here, he's there, he's everywhere, the good, ole Houston Hacker. But mostly, he's right under your big cop noses. I'll be cutting a new gal real soon. Like this weekend, maybe. I dedicate the corpse-to-be to you folks, Houston's finest. Until then, don't take any wooden intestines when I can offer you the real, warm, wet thing.

> Your Pal,
> *THE HACKER*

P.S. I hope you don't find the signature too informal. But I do think Barlowe's *The Houston Hacker* is a bit overdone. Don't you?

PART TWO:
THE BEAST HAS TEETH

. . . I will do such things —
What they are yet I know not — but they shall be
The terrors of the earth.
— *William Shakespeare (**King Lear**)*

The murderer's curse,
　　The dead man's fix'd still
　　　　glare,
And fears, and death's cold
　　　　sweat —
They all are there!
　　—Dana

There is such a thing as the pressure of darkness.
— *Victor Hugo*

Hacker in pieces in blood . . .
　　*From **The Egyptian Book of the Dead***

1

FRIDAY . . . 6:30 p.m.

He unlocked his apartment and went into darkness and loneliness. The light switch could relieve the darkness, but what could relieve the loneliness? So far he had found only one thing: The gushing of blood, the ripping of flesh. Somehow, that did it. It satisfied deep in his gut the same way ejaculation satisfied. It gave him the urge to carry on, gave him strength, like some marvelous elixir brewed by the gods.

Originally he had suppressed his urges, absorbed himself in his job. He was damn good at his job, it put a blanket on his passions. But the dreams became less and less satisfying. Dogs and cats didn't suffer enough. They took their doom too stoically. The job became an intrusion instead of a diversion. It was the sort of job where you were acquainted constantly with death. And each time the urge grew stronger within . . . until there was no other thought but death.

Death!

The mere thought of it brought terror to the hearts of most. For him, it had replaced the word love. It had been that way since his early teens. (Thank you, Doris Johnston.) But he had denied it. Felt as if he and his thoughts were out of place. Unusual, yes. But out of place? Not in the least. From now on he was the elite. Death was his god and the bringing of death was his equivalent of prayer. I am the new Messiah. I bring a new doctrine. Not one of love and peace. But one of death and destruction.

Let there be blood!

He didn't bother with the light switch. He would need a short nap; something to give him strength for later. His mind would need to be sharp, sharp as his blade. He went to his wall bed and pulled it down, threw himself across it. He closed his eyes and determined himself to sleep approximately an hour. The ability to sleep an almost given time was something he had trained himself to do. In his job you had to be ready to go at any moment. You had to learn to sleep when you had the chance.

After a moment he drifted into a semiconscious state where the life he had lived and the life he intended to live walked with entwined fingers. One of his dreamworld inhabitants was Doris Johnston, his first love. And still he loved her. She had been beautiful. Long and sleek with dark brown hair and big, soft, puppy eyes of gold-flecked brown. He had never touched her . . . alive.

He could remember when he asked her for a date. It was as clear as yesterday. She had been wearing a yellow dress. It was short. Her legs were very dark, very beautiful. The hose she wore made them darker, sleeker, sexier.

He had been at his best. Clean body, clean hair, clean clothes; his best clothes — a red and blue short-sleeve, western-cut shirt and crisp blue jeans with plenty of blue still in them. His black wingtips were polished to gun metal brightness.

Simple words in front of her locker at school. He had asked her out. A movie, he remembered. She had turned him down, and not gently. He remembered how he had suddenly felt in his simple clothes. Neat at first, but with her denial, cheap. Like a sorry, plastic product all spiffed up with spit and polish and bright red paint, but still a cheap product; a two dollar Japanese camera in a roadside gift shop stuffed full of brittle peanut candy, miniature cactus and highway maps.

But fate works its little surprises. Less than a week later, while crossing the highway, a carload of drunks ran a red light and came down on her car like a blazing meteor and crushed her beautiful face into her steering wheel.

He remembered the funeral. All tears, flowers and regrets. Mostly young men regretting that such a ripe and lovely piece of ass was no longer among the living and the ready. But it had not been that way with him. He had truly loved her. Deep down and rock hard. And now that she was meat on the mortician's table, and soon to be a cold, white body in the dank, cold ground, he loved her no less.

That was when the compulsion grew. He knew that she was his slave in death. She could no longer deny him her love. She had no say in the matter.

He still remembered the moon. Full and staring down with a milky eye; like an eye made blind by a wound. Like a dog he had once had. A black cur with one hang-down ear and a bleached out eye. An eye like the moon that night. Blind. Staring. Uncaring.

Then there had been the tombstones rising in the darkness like soldiers in crisp white uniforms. But they were lousy sentries. He set his box of tools by the grave (he had stolen them from his uncle, the old tight wad), and with the shovel he began to dig in the still loose dirt. He dug down to the shiny, blue metal coffin, and down in the grave with the box of tools, he opened it and dragged out the swollen, mashed body of Doris.

At the graveside, in the soft dirt, he had raped the body with an inhuman force of will. With his knife he had carved it into a masterpiece of hard, dead flesh. When he had finished, he returned the body — piece by piece — to the coffin and filled in the grave. All except the head. He took that with him. He kept it buried in the field behind his house, in a shallow grave of sweet loam next to the creek. He put a large rock over the small grave to keep out animals. He slid the trowel just under the edge of the rock. He urinated on the grave because he had once read that animals were reluctant to bother anything another animal (human or otherwise) had marked with its urine. He didn't know if this was true or not, and he didn't really care. It gave him a strange satisfaction to whizz his steaming water on the site.

Nightly he rose from his bed and worked his window up. Then, silently, he made his way to the creek bank. Not that he really needed to be stealthy. His mother slept like an anvil when she wasn't entertaining some fat john whose wife was on her period or blessed with the nightly headache. He never could understand why anyone would pay her for what she had to offer. Often he left to the sound of the bedsprings in the next room rising to fever pitch above the lustful gruntings of the john and the uninspired moans of his flatbacking mother.

He would make his way to the creek bank and remove Doris' head from the grave. He would then hold it in his arms and press his lips to her hamburgered lips and toil his tongue against her dirt caked teeth. Then he would place the mashed head at his feet, look down into her eyeless, maggot-infested face and masturbate, ejaculate his sperm on the ruined skull.

When his ritual was finished, he would return the head to the grave, replace the rock and trowel and make his way home. If home is what you call four walls and a bed. It was a place to eat and sleep, nothing more.

When the head was little more than bleached bone and nauseous odor (the smell was like perfume to him), he buried it for good. Deep, and with the rock pressed firmly on top.

No one ever knew the body had been touched. No one ever suspected, not even those who worked attending the graves at the cemetery. He had been careful to put the dirt back carefully and expertly. And with the head buried deep and the rock in place above it, it too was safe from discovery.

He tried to forget the ruined face of Doris. He could not. It came to him in dreams. The dead were his people, and he would bring new disciples to his fold.

He had been careless with the nigger bitch. He had known his victim would be from The Ward — he had been determined to erase his childhood fears of the area — but he had not planned his movements in great detail. He had stolen the car and picked his victim at random, surprised her, forced her into the alley.

But from now on he would pick them with care, learn their habits, their names . . . just like the long-legged blonde girl he had been following this week. Evelyn. Lovely Evelyn.

Thinking of her, he slipped from the semiconscious state and descended into the world of dreams.

He was bathing. Not in water but in blood, urine and feces. He was in a massive, deep tub. He washed himself all over with the gore and waste, rubbed it in his hair, submerged himself, sank deep down into its depths, tasted it, filled his eyes with it . . .

. . . why the tub was on a main street. Women were passing by. Women wearing only panties and high platform shoes. The panties were all the colors of the rainbow. The women all looked like Evelyn; tall, blonde, with tanned, muscular legs. They were all passing by and looking at him.

One stopped and kicked off her shoes, removed her white panties, dropped them in the tub. The panties saturated, became heavy and sank. She turned her back to him, squatted with her ass over the rim of the tub . . . she was peeing on him, peeing all over his face. The other women, all looking like Evelyn, surrounded the tub to watch.

And the urine was turning to blood.

Refreshed, like a vampire rising for his nightly feast, he awoke. He checked his watch.

7:38.

Very good. He had a little over an hour before Evelyn was out of her night class. Plenty of time.

A sudden passion, like a cold chill, raced up his spine. His hands began to quiver with anticipation.

"Soon," he said aloud. "Soon, sweet Evelyn. Soon."

2

FRIDAY . . . 9:18 p.m.

Late classes were a drag. Of that one thing Evelyn DeMarka was certain. But it seemed to her most anything besides the disco was boring these days. Work as a secretary all day long and learn accounting all night long. Christ! This growing up was for the birds.

Evelyn parked her Plymouth in the lot of the Western Division Apartments, got out and started up the walk.

There was one reprieve from all this work, she reminded herself as she neared the metal stairs that led up to her second floor apartment. There was a hot shower, coffee, and at eleven Frank would be by. Tonight they would have fun in the sack, watch the late, late show — providing they weren't still supplying their own superior entertainment — and then tomorrow they could go on the picnic they had been planning; top it all off with a night at The Lost Weekend Disco.

Yep, that was the game plan. Then Sunday they could rest. She might even be able to talk Frank into moving in . . .

She heard a noise, slowed her pace.

Nothing. She didn't hear a thing now.

She started walking again. She was almost to the stairs.

The trashcans beneath the stairs rattled.

Evelyn stopped, tucked her books up tight beneath her arm, listened.

No other sound came to her ears. A cat she decided. Simple as that, a cat in the garbage. She started up the stairs briskly.

There was a jerk at her ankle.

She screamed. The books and papers she was carrying went flying and she toppled backwards. Just before her back hit the bottom step she realized what had occurred. *Someone had reached through the steps and grabbed her ankle. Someone hiding in the shadows. Someone with a grip like iron.*

The step striking her back sent an explosive pain throughout her body. It felt as if the world's population were wearing cleats and walking up and down her spine.

She opened her mouth to scream again. A voice, hard as flint, cold as ice, said: "Scream again, and I cut your heart out."

Evelyn held her scream. She could see a face now, peering between the steps. The eyes were like those of some demon. The arm of the man was fully stretched through the stairs, his gloved hand clutching her ankle tightly.

"I warn you," the chilling voice said again, "don't scream."

She could see more of the man now. There was something in his other hand. He was holding it up for her to see. It looked like a sword there in the shadows.

"Oh God!" she said trying to twist free.

The man let go of her ankle, came around the stairs quickly, buried his fingers in her hair.

Evelyn saw that he was wearing a raincoat. That was crazy, she thought; it didn't even look like rain.

"Get up, cunt!" he said, pulling her down the last three steps 'til she lay on her back at the base of the stairs. He tugged her upright by her hair, pressing the point of the bayonet against her spine. "One scream and I run the bayonet all the way through, my pretty."

"You're . . . you're him. The one in the papers," she said softly.

"You mean," he held the last words for effect, "The Hacker?"

Evelyn could not speak. She just nodded.

"No. Not me, Evelyn."

"How . . . how do you know my name?"

"I know lots of things. I'm observant. You should learn to be. You might have saved yourself this night had you been observant. Women aren't real bright, are they, Evelyn?"

Evelyn said nothing. Her breathing was labored. Her back felt like a river of molten lava. The point of the bayonet wasn't helping any.

"You didn't answer me, Evelyn. Women aren't too bright, are they?"

"No."

"No what?"

"Wo . . . women aren't too bright."

"Good, good. You're not too bright, right, Evelyn?"

"No. No, I'm not too bright."

"I'm a man in need of a little, hot, tight pussy. You got hot tight pussy, Evelyn?"

Evelyn swallowed.

"Up the stairs, sweetheart."

Sobbing. "Don't hurt me. God, don't hurt me."

"Evelyn. Such lack of trust."

"Please."

"Up the stairs. And keep it quiet, or I'll hurt you."

"I'll do as you say."

"I know."

"You won't hurt me?"

"Wouldn't think of it. Come on, Evelyn. Up the stairs. Let's go to your place for a little fun."

They went upstairs. She unlocked the apartment for him.

"Just a little fun, Evelyn. Just a little fun."

Evelyn had no fun at all.

FRIDAY . . . 11:01 p.m.

Frank Callahan, Evelyn DeMarka's steady boyfriend, first felt fear when he found the books and papers at the bottom of the stairs. Friday night they had a steady date as soon as he was off work. Talk, sex and the late movie. A nice combination. It had gone that way for months. He looked forward to it. It made his Fridays.

He wasn't so sure right now. Something was churning in his guts. He couldn't imagine why Evelyn's books — correction — he could imagine why her books were where they were. He could imagine all sorts of things. What he wanted to imagine was a rational explanation for the books, but he couldn't. He tried a few, but none stuck to his brain.

He went up the stairs with the key Evelyn had given him in his hand. Normally he knocked in spite of the key, but tonight the door had no life. He feared he would knock and she would not answer. The door gave him the same feel he got from old, vacant, boarded up houses, an almost supernatural feel of gloom and depression.

I'm being silly, he told himself. Silly. There's a rational

explanation for those books being where they are, and Evelyn will give it to me and we'll laugh, and afterwards we'll have sex and feel great.

Why did the thoughts ring hollow in his mind?

He slipped the key into the lock. It snicked free. He turned the knob and made silent prayer as he opened the door — to whom he prayed he was uncertain since he was an atheist — but for some reason, it seemed the thing to do.

It'll be all right, he told himself. It'll be all right, it'll be all right, it'll be all right, it'll be all right.

Frank went in.

It was not all right.

SATURDAY . . . 1:15 a.m.

He wiped the bayonet off with a damp rag, then used a dry towel. He inspected it for rust. Not a spot. Not even a fleck. He would sharpen it tomorrow.

The one tonight had dulled it. She had certainly had tough bone, but not a lot of spirit. In fact, she hardly had any spirit at all. He put the bundled raincoat in the sink and removed tonight's morsel.

"And they say I'm heartless."

He put it in a plastic container, placed it in the freezer.

"Talk about a cold, cold heart." He chuckled at his own joke.

He heated water for instant coffee. He had two fig bars with his coffee. After his snack, he took his raincoat to the bathroom, opened it up and stretched it out in the tub. He turned the shower on, watching fascinated, as the blood swirled and bubbled and fled down the drain.

He shook out the raincoat, hung it over the shower curtain rod. He went back to the kitchen to get the sheer plastic gloves he had used tonight. He wrung them out over the kitchen sink, then struck a match and held it to them. The gloves shrunk, made black plastic smoke — the kind that stinks. He loved the odor. It was incense to him.

Part of the gloves wouldn't burn.

Too much blood.

When Frank Callahan found Evelyn he did not call the police. His knees buckled and he collapsed with his back against the wall. He sat there staring catatonically. The only sound he could make was a whimper. In a deep state of shock he sat that way until 4:17. At that time he began to scream bloody murder at the top of his lungs.

Mildred Cofey, the apartment manager, went up to investigate. She was angry and sleepy and determined to throw the troublemaker out on his or her ear. It never occurred to her that the screams were of anguish.

The door to Evelyn DeMarka's apartment was open. Miss Cofey found Frank curled up on the floor crying. She also saw Evelyn and she was suddenly and violently ill all over the carpet that just last week Evelyn had insisted she have shampooed.

Staggering, trying to get away from Frank, whom she thought to be the murderer, Miss Cofey half stumbled downstairs and called the police.

SATURDAY . . . 4:58 a.m.

Two carloads of blue suits and an ambulance came first.

The officers checked out the area and sealed off the room.

Frank Callahan, hysterical, had been hauled away in the ambulance when Hanson arrived. Clark came fifteen minutes later, the lab boys shortly thereafter.

It was Hanson's and Clark's baby now, even if it was no longer in The Ward. Of course other officers and detectives were involved. No policeman works alone like the movies depict, but this case was Hanson's and Clark's main concern. And now, viewing the murder scene and the body — what was left of it — Hanson determined that The Hacker would be caught, and by him. He also determined that when he caught the beast, he would make sure that the guy had a little accident on the way to the station. He felt certain that The Hacker would choose to do something rash. Like make a run for it. Hanson intended to give him a warning shot in the back of the head.

The bed where the bulk of her lay was dark with blood. Her head, fingers and feet were missing. The head was found in the toilet bowl; blonde hair matted strawberry red, eyeless, noseless, lipless. Her fingers had been chopped off and arranged in a row on the kitchen sink. Her feet had been amputated and placed beneath the bed. Intestines were strung out over the room, draped over the bedroom light fixture and the bed post. The smell was awful.

Cameras flashed as police photographers made their pictures. The lab crew went about their duties. Voices, usually buzzing at even the most brutal of crimes, were oddly silent. The men and women of the homicide team were all pale faced, except for Hanson, and as black as he was, it was hard to tell. But his eyes were wide and his pupils were dilated.

Death, Hanson thought, I never get used to it. No one that's human gets used to it. Not a cop, a fireman or an ambulance driver. You accept it. You adjust quicker and easier than the average man or woman whose closest exposure to death was their Aunt Minnie's funeral; the memory of it a hazy blur of peaceful features and white face made "life-like" by makeup. You might even crack jokes about it, but adjust or not, you did not get used to it. At least not if you were normal. Or unless you were The

Hacker.

Hanson said softly, "Joe, I'm gonna get this fucker. I'm gonna make sure he has a little accident on the way to the station."

Clark moved up close to Hanson. "Not so loud. They already think we're a bunch of thugs."

Hanson turned to him. "They?"

"The papers. The people."

"Just cops here."

"Just best to be quiet. Keep it down and the people and the papers never know. I mean Barlowe's contact might be right here in the room."

"Fuckum."

"That's who we work for, Gorilla. The people, remember? You and I, we're the good guys."

"We're not trying to drown handcuffed Mexicans or play Russian roulette with some black kid in the back seat of a cop car. We're trying to get ourselves a cold-blooded looney. No insanity plea for him. No nice, cozy cell and hot meals. No psychiatrist telling him it's all because he had poor potty training as a child. I'm gonna get this motherfucker. With you or without you. I don't want anyone else to get him. I want to get him. *I mean really get him.*"

"Easy, man."

"Easy, hell!"

A lab technician turned to look at them.

Clark rested his hand on Hanson's elbow. Hanson pulled away from him, stalked outside the apartment, away from the smell of horrible death. Clark did not follow.

Hanson stood at the top of the stairs and looked out over the city. Daylight was creeping in. Electric lights were dying.

Hanson rubbed his huge hands across his eyes, up and over his forehead. Saturday morning a corpse for breakfast, he thought. What a way to start a day. What a way to make a living. There wasn't even a goddamned skyline to look at. Just grey and black smog rising above the city, eating away what would normally have been a beautiful morning blue. But nothing was normal anymore. Nothing.

Or worse yet, maybe there was a new kind of normalcy. A normalcy made up of sickness, death and despair. And this Hacker, this motherfuckin' Hacker, was its High Priest.

Well, watch out Priest of Blood. Watch out. 'Cause Marvin Hanson is gonna blow your ass away.

3

MONDAY

Barlowe's Monday morning column no longer walked the line between journalism and sensationalism. It had leaped feet first into melodrama and exaggeration, although the latter was a bit hard to accomplish in as gruesome a case as the death of Evelyn DeMarka.

The article took its toll. People were afraid to walk the streets after dark. Shopping malls suffered. Movie theaters remained half filled. Waitresses leaned on bars and sat at tables and looked out at the night, not looking forward to walking to their cars. Cars growled along the highway with windows rolled up tight and doors locked and respectable speeds maintained. Lights burned in houses and apartments far beyond normal hours. And those who lived alone lived enveloped in double terror.

The city had cold chills and goosebumps. The Hacker stalked the streets of Houston, and no one was anxious to become his next victim. The week began to slink by on coward's feet.

But The Hacker knew there would always be victims. The world would not crawl into a hole and pull the hole in behind it. There would be others to cut; others to drip blood and guts. Women were such fools, just a little time and they'd stick their noses outdoors again, and soon thereafter they'd be flaunting their stuff again; teasing him, tormenting him.

But now it was his turn to torment back. His turn to hand out agony and fear like party favors, and he had a mental sack full.

Sleep was hard for him anymore. His dreams kept him awake with anticipation. He needed his bloody elixir for peace of mind and relaxation of the body, and he needed it more often.

He awakened almost every hour on the hour and listened to his old-fashioned, wind-up alarm clock tick heavily in the emptiness of his dingy room. The bed and the sheets stank of sweat where he had tossed and turned. He drifted in and out of sleep, and shortly before daybreak he arose, went to the bathroom to relieve himself. He washed his hands afterwards and looked in the cracked mirror over his rust stained sink for a long, somber moment; the crack sliced his face from forehead to jaw.

Face.

God! Sometimes he couldn't focus; couldn't even remember what he looked like. Was the mirror filled with a stranger? Sometimes it seemed that way, seemed that the face looking out of that cheap, cracked mirror was not his at all. Sometimes this body he wore didn't even seem his. It was as if someone else lived in this plaster peeling dump over the rooms of old women who creaked worse than his rusted bedsprings. It was as if his mind were trapped in a robot's body, and that body did as it pleased in spite of how his mind thought.

And then . . . other times it was just the reverse. It was his mind that had control, and the robot was merely a slave . . .

Whatever the function, he constantly felt outside himself; a half separate entity from that thing that looked at him from the mirror.

He washed his face and went back to bed.

After awhile his mind dove into the dreaming pleasure of gurgling blood and cold death; and this time, it helped him sleep.

Rachel, feeling uneasy, awoke.

Hanson was not beside her. It didn't seem that he had been to bed at all. She worked vision into her eyes and sat up. When she felt oriented she swung her legs over the side of the bed and slipped on her houseshoes. She plucked her robe from a chair and put it on. Quietly, she opened the bedroom door and stepped out into the hallway. She went to the head of the stairs and looked down into the dining room below. There wasn't a light on, nor was there a sliver of illumination beneath the door to the den. If he was up, he wasn't reading. She pulled the robe tight about her and went downstairs.

She went first to the kitchen. Nothing.

The dining room. Nothing.

The den. Nothing.

Puzzled, she stared back through the house, stopped when she heard the doorknob rattle in the living room; the door to the outside.

"Marvin?" she said, and the moment the word passed her lips she felt foolish. She had said it much too softly for anyone to hear. She could barely hear it herself.

She went into the living room.

The door was opening, a man's outline was in the doorway.

"Marvin?"

"Yes."

Rachel let out her breath with a loud sigh.

Hanson shut the door, flicked the lock. He flicked on a light. Rachel, a faint smile of relief on her face, had a bit more cream mixed in her chocolate color than usual.

"Honey, what's the matter?"

"Just scared me. I saw you weren't in bed, and . . . " She waved her arms expansively.

"Hey, I'm sorry. I didn't mean to scare you."

"Of course not."

"You shouldn't be up. You," Hanson looked at his watch, "hell, woman, you go to work in a couple of hours."

"It's all right."

"No, it's not. It's my fault."

"You don't ask for the hours they give you."

Hanson looked sheepish. "My own hours. I got home hours

ago. I couldn't sleep. I'm sorry, baby."

"All right. It's all right." Her voice wasn't ecstatic with pleasure in spite of her words. Rachel highly valued her sleep.

"I just couldn't sleep."

"You're going to feel like hell today."

"I know."

"Where you been, Marve?"

"Walking."

Rachel went to him, they embraced. "What's the matter, baby?"

"Old age, I guess. Can't sleep."

"You're not so old . . . Not from what I can tell." She gave him a lecherous wink.

He smiled. "How would you know? We don't have time for that anymore."

Rachel made a pouty expression. "True. Long as we're up, want some coffee?"

"Sure."

Rachel kissed him on the cheek. "I'll make some." She started for the kitchen.

"Baby?" Hanson said.

Rachel turned. "Yes?"

"I'm sorry about waking you up."

"You didn't wake me."

"I mean about not being there and all. In bed."

She winked at him. "I'll make the coffee."

Hanson went to the window, pulled the curtains back. He

looked out at the street and the houses nestled quietly across the way. Rachel started up the Mr. Coffee machine, came back and put her arms around Hanson.

"Where'd you walk?"

Hanson let the curtain drop. "Just down the sidewalk and on out to the highway. It's a beautiful night."

"What were you thinking about?"

"Nothing much."

"The Hacker?" Rachel asked softly.

"Yeah."

"It's eating you up. Why? Why is this one so personal?"

"I don't know. I guess because it's everything I'm against." He turned into her arms and held her.

"Let's go to bed."

"It's almost daylight. Been up this long I might as well stay up."

"Who said anything about sleeping."

"Ah, dark designs. What about the coffee?"

"It'll turn off and be nice and hot when we're ready."

"I'm getting nice and hot now."

"And I'm ready."

They went upstairs.

MONDAY AFTERNOON

He left work early that day with sickness as the cause. He went to his apartment and tried to sleep. He managed a couple of hours before the whine of the garbage compactor brought him awake. Giving up on sleep, he went to the flyspecked window and looked out. After a moment he raised the window and pushed the stick that held it up in place. He listened to the clang and clatter of the garbage truck; the banging of the garbage cans and the talk of the sanitation men at work. It was getting along toward evening, going from grey to black with wavey fingers of pink still sticking out like pulsing veins.

The city. The crawling, clanging, banging city.

The sour contents of the garbage truck drifted to his nostrils; vomit, baby diapers, stinking Kotex, mildewed underwear and all manner of food slop filled his head with its odor.

He loved it. The smell was nectar. And slowly, his element, the night came; crawling, black velvet full of city sounds and city smells . . . and like free diamonds lying on the velvet darkness, were the women. Whores, each and every last one of them. And if he could, if there was that much time in a night, he would pluck them all from the velvet and leave its fabric blank of sparkle and full only of darkness . . . and red, red blood.

But he must have patience. The city was on guard tonight. He must wait until it jerked its latch and threw open its doors. Then, when they least expected it . . . he would strike.

TUESDAY . . . 11:15 a.m.

Tuesday, Philip Barlowe began a series about murders similar to those of The Hacker. He drew parallels. Joe Clark read the column carefully. When he finished, he cut it out and put it in the desk drawer with the others.

Hanson, who was once again typing out reports in his stutter style method, said, "You still reading those?"

"It has to do with the case, doesn't it?"

"Pretty vaguely."

"Part of being a good cop. You want to see that list they gave me when I was taking criminology?"

"What list?"

"The list that tells what makes up a good investigator."

"You're kidding?"

"Nope. Want to see?"

"Not particularly."

Undaunted, Clark went around to the desk drawer again and dug down deep, came up with a purple folder full of papers.

"Christ," Hanson said. "Is that the list?"

"Not all these papers . . . they're related, but . . ." Clark opened the folder and took out the top sheet of paper. "Look at this."

"Shit."

"Just for the hell of it."

"All right. Give it to me."

The list read:

1. SUSPICION
2. CURIOSITY
3. OBSERVATION
4. MEMORY
5. ORDINARY INTELLIGENCE AND COMMON SENSE
6. UNBIASED AND UNPREJUDICED MIND
7. AVOIDANCE OF INACCURATE CONCLUSIONS
8. PATIENCE, UNDERSTANDING, COURTESY
9. ABILITY TO PLAY A ROLE
10. ABILITY TO GAIN AND HOLD CONFIDENCE
11. PERSISTENCE AND TIRELESS CAPACITY FOR WORK
12. A KNOWLEDGE OF THE CORPUS DELICTI OF CRIMES
13. AN INTEREST IN SOCIOLOGY AND PSYCHOLOGY
14. ABILITY TO RECOGNIZE PERSONS WHO ARE LIKELY TO BE THE SUBJECT OF POLICE INVESTIGATIONS
15. RESOURCEFULNESS
16. KNOWLEDGE OF INVESTIGATIVE TECHNIQUES
17. ABILITY TO MAKE FRIENDS AND SECURE THE COOP-

ERATION OF OTHERS
18. TACT, SELF CONTROL AND DIGNITY
19. INTEREST IN JOB AND PRIDE OF ACCOMPLISHMENT
20. LOYALTY

Hanson handed Clark back the list.

"Well?" Clark asked.

"Well what?"

"What do you think?"

"Pretty good," Hanson admitted grudgingly. "Seems right. I never thought about what it took for an investigator, but that's pretty close. One more maybe. Gut instinct. You've either got it or you don't."

"Agreed," Clark said, nodding.

"Wait a minute," Hanson said, "you're trying to tell me something."

"Remember what we were talking about. I collect those columns because I'm," Clark looked at the list, "number two, curious."

"That's an odd way to make a point."

"Yeah. Do you remember number eighteen?"

"No."

"Tact, self-control and dignity."

"So."

"So you're taking this all too much to heart, Gorilla. It's eating your insides out."

"You're starting to sound like Rachel."

"Listen to the woman. She know of what she speaks."

116

"Bullshit!"

"Just promise me you'll try to take it easy."

"This is crazy."

"Promise me you'll take it easy. I don't need a partner with an ulcer."

Hanson sighed. "All right. I know when I'm whipped. I promise to try."

"Good."

"Man, you college folks sure do go a long way to make a point."

"Yeah, we're a real pain in the ass sometimes."

"Most of the time."

"Humm . . . Oh, say, Gorilla."

"Now what?"

"When do I get my very own desk?"

"You don't."

"Oh."

WEDNESDAY . . . 10:15 a.m.

Barlowe's typing sounded like machine gun fire. Ratatattat, ratatattat, ratatattat.

A feminine voice interrupted his progress with, "Philip?"

Barlowe looked up from his work. "Yes?"

Sharon Carson, the attractive brunette receptionist, stood over him, a long, blue envelope in her hand.

"I found this on the desk a moment ago. It's addressed to you, but I don't remember seeing anyone put it there. Maybe when I went to the water fountain . . ."

"Put it down!" Barlowe snapped.

"What?"

"Put it down," he said more gently. "Excuse me for being so sharp, Sharon. But I think it might be from *him*."

"Him . . . The . . . The Hacker?"

Barlowe nodded.

Sharon put the envelope on his desk as if it were a fragile Ming Dynasty Vase. "Christ, I never . . ."

"No sweat. It might be a bill."

"It doesn't have a return address on it."

"Yeah. The last one was in an envelope just like this. Thanks, Sharon. I'll handle it from here."

"Okay. Man, I'm sorry."

"Forget it. Go on back to work. I'll take care of it."

Sharon, feeling as inadequate as the proverbial tits on a boar hog, went back to her desk. She watched tight faced from there while Barlowe, using a folded sheet of typing paper, picked up the letter in its groove and carried it into the office of the editor, Evans.

"Chief," Barlowe said opening the door.

Evans, a white-haired, plump-faced man with a body to match the face, looked up at Barlowe. "Yes." There was a scowl on his face and impatience in his voice. "What is it?"

"This," Barlowe said dumping the letter and typing paper on Evan's desk. "Don't touch it, Chief."

Evans withdrew the hand he had been snaking toward the letter. Recognition crossed his face. "Him?"

"I think so. Sharon brought it to me. She found it on the main desk . . . just lying there. She didn't see who brought it in. One thing for sure. It didn't come in with the morning mail. There's no stamp."

"I see that. I guess he just waltzed in and put the goddamned thing on the desk himself."

Barlowe licked his lips. "Looks that way . . . if it's him. I've got a feeling it is. I mean it does look like the last one. The blue envelope and all. My name on the front in carefully cut letters. Who else could it be?"

"Yeah."

"Should we open it?"

"I don't think so. I'm calling the cops. Let them decide what to do."

"It might turn out to be a note from one of my police informers."

"Then that's the breaks. The cat's out of the bag. Better that than us ruining evidence."

"Yeah. I guess you're right . . . Besides, it's just like the last one."

"It's him. I bet you my job. Sit down, Phil." Evans waved him at a chair. Barlowe sat. Evans pushed buttons on his phone.

Fifteen minutes later the police were there.

Wearing sheer plastic gloves, Hanson opened the small blade of his pocket knife and cut one end of the envelope open. He pinched out the letter inside. It was typed on one sheet of typing paper, single space.

Clark, standing at his side, said, "I guess he got tired of cutting out paper. Maybe the typewriter will give us a lead."

"I bet not," Hanson said sourly.

"What does it say?" Evans said, a bit surprised at his loss of self-control, a trait with which he prided himself.

Hanson read it out loud, softly.

This line sung to the tune of "Fun, Fun, Fun," by the Beach Boys. "Gonna hack, hack, hack 'til the cops take my bayonet away." And I may have fun indefinitely at the rates those fools work. I sent this note to you, Barlowe, because I kind of like your reporting. Good, sensational stuff you write. Tell the cops this: I'm gonna hack and rip all I can. I'm gonna cut every woman I can find from gut to gill. They're gonna suffer. Think about that. Think about it real hard. It could be your sister, your lover, your wife, or even your mother. And it'll be me, old Houston Hacker, leaning over them with my sharp blade and rising passion. And let me tell you, I am passionate. I love my work and I want *Blood!*
THE HACKER

When Hanson finished Barlowe said, "Christ!"

Hanson folded the note, returned it to the envelope. He gave the envelope to Clark, removed his gloves and stuffed them in his coat pocket. He said to Barlowe:

"I hold you half responsible for this."

Barlowe frowned. "What in the fuck are you talking about?"

"The sensationalist crap you write. Just like it said in the goddamned note. He likes it. That's what drives him on, keeps him killing."

"Preposterous!" Evans said.

Hanson ignored him, continued talking to Barlowe. "An ego, Barlowe, a goddamned, warped ego is what keeps him going. And you're helping the sick bastard satisfy it."

"Easy, Gorilla," Clark said.

"I just print the facts," Barlowe said. "What I write doesn't make him kill."

"Sure," Hanson snapped. "Just the facts."

Clark took hold of Hanson's arm. He could feel the muscles knotting through Hanson's jacket. Any minute he expected Hanson to lunge at the reporter.

"Come on," Clark said gently. "Enough."

Barlowe's grey eyes were churning with anger. "You can't talk to me like that."

"I just did," Hanson said.

Nervously, Barlowe pushed his long blond hair out of his eyes. His knees were quivering. Clark wasn't sure if it was from fear or anger.

"You're doing your job, I'm doing mine," Barlowe said.

"Yeah," Hanson growled.

"Look," Evans said. "You get your ass out of here . . . or. . . "

"Or what?" Hanson said giving Evans a sour look. "You'll call the police? Is that it?"

"No. Guess not," Evans said. "The police are a bunch of hoodlums."

"Uh huh. And you folks are a bunch of swell guys," Hanson said.

"Take it easy," Clark said again. He still held Hanson's arm.

Hanson pulled his arm free, snarled, "Shut up, Joe." Then to Evans and Barlowe, "You folks just print the facts, huh. Sit in your offices and lay the news on the line. Well, we're the ones that have to deal with the nuts. We have to take the abuse . . . and you give the public blood. You people are sicker even than the goddamned Hacker."

Clark grabbed Hanson's arm again, half tugged him to the door. Hanson protested at first, but after a moment relented. Clark opened the door and pulled Hanson out of the office and into the sound of a dozen typewriters. He closed the door so Evans and Barlowe couldn't hear.

"Are you nuts?" Clark said flatly.

"Maybe," Hanson said.

"I don't doubt it none. Listen to me, man. We don't need the press against us. Got me?"

Hanson didn't say anything.

"You're the one that taught me to keep my cool, to only get tough as a bluff or when you really had to. Neither rule applies here. You're just plain being a horse's ass."

Hanson took in a deep breath. "Yeah, I know . . . It's getting to me, Joe."

"Why now? I mean do you think I like to see those hacked bodies?"

"Of course not."

"You're the senior officer. You're my example. Now pull yourself together."

Hanson ran his hand over his forehead and into his hair.

"Well?" Clark said.

"I'm together."

"You're sure?"

"I'm sure."

Clark smiled. "Remember. It's you black folks that are cool. Us honkeys are excitable. Got it?"

"Yeah, I got it."

"I'd apologize if I were you."

"What? Oh come on, Joe." Hanson's voice was back up to shouting level again.

Clark said calmly, "Looks damn tacky for the cops to spend all their time shouting at one another."

Hanson noticed that the typewriters had stopped. People were watching them.

"You're right," Hanson said calmly. "I lost my head. I'm not going to like this, but you're right. I'm being a horse's ass."

"And doing an A-One job of it, I might add."

"Guess so."

"No guess. You are. Come on, let's go back inside."

The typewriter symphony started up again.

Clark opened the door and Hanson went in first. Hanson's apology was brief and to the point. Evans and Barlowe accepted, made some feeble apologies themselves. No one's heart was in it.

Clark did most of the questioning of Barlowe and Evans after that. Hanson went out to interview Sharon Carson who had discovered the note. It was his method of getting away from Evans and Barlowe gracefully. He asked Carson several questions. She tried, but none of her answers were very helpful.

4

WEDNESDAY . . . 11:45 a.m.

When Hanson and Clark left *The Bugle*, Evans and Barlowe went to the lunchroom for coffee. Two years back the paper barely had enough room for a coffee break. Now it was successful enough to provide a lunchroom with machine-served food; it didn't taste like mama's, but it was a long way from the old one-room newspaper office.

Over a cup of coffee Barlowe said, "You think I'm overdoing it, Chief?"

"Overdoing what?" Evans asked around a mouthful of ham sandwich.

"You know, the Hacker stuff."

"You're doing your job."

"The column's all right, then?"

"It's all right," Evans replied with his usual impatience. "It sells papers, don't it?"

"That's not what I meant. Personally. Now tell me honest, don't hold any punches. What do you think? You think maybe I'm overdoing it? Tell me honest now."

Evans gulped down another mouthful of sandwich, leaned back in his chair and placed his hands on his ample belly. "Phil," he said, "We get along together, right? I mean we aren't bosom buddies, but then neither of us are exactly the best company in the world. We're too damn driven. We're newspaper men. We live it, breathe it, shit it. Right?"

Barlowe nodded.

"You worked your way up to that column. Started with obits. Hell, no way you're going to forget that."

"No way is right." Barlowe smiled. "I remember once you told me if there ain't nobody dead, go out and kill somebody, but fill that column."

This time Evans smiled. It looked like it really hurt him. "I remember," Evans said. "You earned that column you got. It's the most popular thing in the paper. I'll admit it's a little different, not really journalistic in format and presentation, but we didn't start at the heights, boy. Something about your style appealed to me."

"That's sort of what I mean. I mean . . . "

"You mean is that old black fart right about us making people go dingo?"

"Yeah."

126

"No. He isn't right. Your column is more graphic than most, but compared to books and movies these days it's as tame as my Aunt Martha's rabbits . . . That's not a cut. I'm just saying that for a newspaper of our kind that column is perfect. That what you wanted to hear?"

"I suppose."

Evans made with the painful smile again. "Remember the first time you came to me with the idea for the column?"

"Sure. I was scared to death."

"That you were. But I liked the idea then and I like it now. I'll be frank as shit with you, son. The paper wasn't doing worth a frog fart 'til you started up that column. It wasn't much at first, but it was novel, and it led to other ideas. Look at all the columns we have now, even that short story page . . . I mean all that came directly from the success of *The Crime Scene*. It fostered the others. It's the big papa. I'm the editor of this rag. I pay your salary. That should be answer enough. If I thought you were hurting *The Bugle*, or if I thought your work was horseshit, I'd tell you. You know goddamned good and well that I would. Right?"

"Right."

"All right. Now the hell with worrying about it. You keep on diggin' dirt, and keep on writing your column, and let me keep you in line. Right now I think you're doing a hell of a fine job . . . and Phil?"

"Yeah."

Evans rubbed his chin with thumb and forefinger, he was smiling again, and this time the operation looked painless. "I think your next column should have something in it about the visit we got from the cops; something about that big coon blowing his stack. Remember as much of that note as you can. I can help you some since I've got a good memory for things like that, and run that in your column, too. Play up the angle on how frustrated the fuzz are."

"Gotcha. And no problem on the note. I damn near have a photographic memory . . . and better yet, I have contacts at the police station. My main contact, the one that's been helping me on The Hacker stuff, is set for an appointment today."

That was a key sentence, and Evans, from past experience knew it. He took out his wallet, fingered out two twenties and a ten. "Here. Give this to our Deep Throat. That is his usual fee?"

"That's it," Barlowe said, taking the money. "I think I can get him to Xerox the note for me. He works in the Evidence Department."

"Good deal. You play up this sicko good. And don't worry. We're probably helping the police. Negative publicity for the police will get them off their lard butts."

"I'm beginning to wonder if we are dealing with a sicko."

"Huh?"

"I mean, not in the usual sense." Barlowe finished off his coffee. "Maybe this guy is one of those types that doesn't remember he's The Hacker—blacks out, has amnesia afterwards, that sort of thing—but I don't think so. His notes are too damn calculating, taunting. I think maybe he's a new breed of man. A sort of social mutant."

Evans finished off the rest of his ham sandwich, rubbed his hands together dusting off the crumbs. "I'm not sure I follow you," he said.

"He's a product of our society. I think he knows exactly what he's doing. He has no remorse. He is not deranged. He is a modern man; a man that can survive in our technological, no-feel society."

"Interesting angle."

"The man behind those notes is cunning and dangerous. A sort of criminal genius, a blood-thirsty Moriarty."

"Genius! I don't think I'd go that far."

"Why not? He plans perfectly. He taunts the police. He leaves notes on our newsdesk, for heaven's sake. I mean that's some kind of gall."

"Gall doesn't make him a genius . . . but it does make him scary."

"True enough. Just a feeling I've got about the guy."

"That's what I like about you, Phil. Feelings. It goes into your work. A good second sense. That's what makes a good newspaperman; someone who can smell the shit beneath the perfume. It isn't made. You're born with it or you aren't."

"Thanks."

Evans threw up his hands in a "nothing to it" gesture. Then: "The cops, bumbling or not, will catch him. A guy like this will go too far eventually. He's too eager to satisfy his lust. He'll fuck up, and when he does, they'll nab him."

"I hope you're right."

"Sure I am."

"Somehow I feel this guy's going to be another Jack the Ripper. He'll pull his crimes and quit without a trace."

"Bet Jack didn't just quit. Something happened to the old boy to stop him. He died, was killed or moved on, something like that. No, once these dingos start they don't quit. They can't quit. Whatever got them going in the first place is still with them, gnawing like a parasite, never stopping until it totally consumes the nut . . . No. He won't just quit."

"Let's hope not. And speaking of cops," Barlowe looked at his watch, "I've got a little meeting with one of the unholy order in about an hour."

"Well," Evans said rising, "no rest for the wicked."

Barlowe pushed back his chair as he stood. "And the good don't need any."

5

WEDNESDAY . . . 12:45 p.m.

Hanson's stomach was doing its wild tiger imitation for the umpteenth time in the last fifteen minutes.

Hanson looked at his watch. Clark had gone for pizza half an hour ago. Christ! The place was just on the corner. Nothing was fast and efficient anymore . . . not even his stomach. It moaned and it churned and it cursed and it flipped and it flopped. But worse yet, when he finished the pizza he would suffer indigestion and heartburn. The price of getting old, he thought. But what the hell. I'll go down with a pepperoni clenched in my teeth.

It was while Hanson was contemplating the condition of his stomach that James Milo from Evidence came up to his desk.

"Milo," Hanson said in way of greeting.

Milo laid a sheet of paper on Hanson's desk. "A note from

Warren. He asked me to drop it off to you since he's out for the rest of the afternoon. I meant to give it to you earlier, forgot."

"No sweat. Haven't been here much today anyway. This and that."

"Well, see you later. I'm going out for lunch."

"And it looks like I'm doing without."

When Milo had departed, Hanson picked up the note and read it:

> Hanson,
>   Have made an examination of Evelyn DeMarka's body. Autopsy report available any time. Work of same man, of course. One thing — clue. Found a button in her split abdomen. It appears to be from something like a raincoat. It's vinyl. Since there are threads still connected to the button, I assume that it came off during the attack on the already dead and ripped corpse. Or perhaps it was placed there on purpose. No telling in a crime like this. I have turned the button into Evidence. Oh yes, the bloody bastard took her heart. But all this is in the report. I just thought the stuff about the button might interest you without having to wade through all the technical bullshit.
>
> > Warren

Hanson folded the note and pushed it under the edge of his typewriter. He thought, a button, huh, a raincoat button. He let the thought circulate, and slowly he began to form a theory.

WEDNESDAY . . . 1:00 p.m.

Sergeant James Milo had an hour for lunch. He didn't intend to eat. He wasn't on a diet. He was on the take. Fifty dollars seemed a better deal to him than a tuna fish sandwich. He could eat later. Right now it was necessary that he meet Barlowe.

The meeting was scheduled at Galleria Mall, inside a busy bookstore. Each meeting was in a different place. Milo insisted on that to avoid a pattern.

Milo browsed the books, unconsciously plucked one from the shelf and pretended to look at it. The book was a quality paperback titled *Vampires*. The cover painting was of a lean, cadaverous man in black, the paleness of his face accented by the blood-red of his lips. Gore leaked from the corner of his mouth and his bloodshot eyes were glazed and extended with lust. A very striking cover. Milo didn't even notice. He flipped through the pages without seeing.

James Milo had been on the Houston Police Force for ten years. If anyone had ever told him that he'd eventually get dirty he would have punched them.

Not anymore.

He began taking graft two years ago. He tried to reconcile that it was due to the fact that his boy was sick. Cerebral palsy was the sort of disease that required considerable medical attention as well as considerable money. The latter being something he had very little of.

He first got dirty with the prostitutes. A few dollars here and there not to squeal on the whores. And what was wrong with that? They were a public service, were they not? Besides, after an arrest they'd be back on the streets in twenty-fours hours, so what did it matter?

Then it was gambling. A few dollars not to mention some of the joints, the ones that paid the best. Gambling wasn't any big deal. It took place right in the heart of the city. Some of the biggest names in Houston were customers to the tables. Hell! Somebody ought to legalize it anyway.

And then there was Barlowe. All he had to do for the reporter was slip him information from time to time out of Evidence. Nothing really major, stuff that didn't make any difference anyway. Besides, Barlowe and his paper paid good money for it. As much as fifty dollars for the smallest of hearsay crumbs. Since The Hacker, Barlowe had been a veritable gold mine.

But Hanson worried him. That guy was suspicious. He hadn't said anything, but Milo knew the guy. He could see it in his eyes. He may not suspect him, just yet, but he did suspect, and eventually it could lead back to him . . . the bad news. It was all getting too warm for comfort, much too warm . . .

"James."

"Wha . . . !" Milo nearly dropped the book. "Barlowe. You scared the shit out of me."

Barlowe looked at the book Milo was holding. "I can imagine, reading that stuff."

Milo grinned lopsided. When he grinned his near-bald head seemed to sag forward. "I wasn't reading. Just flipping the pages. Waiting."

Barlowe pushed his hair out of his eyes, a constant, and to Milo, irritating gesture of his. "Well," the reporter said, "are we going to stand here and try to look casual, or get on with it?"

Milo replaced the book, moved down the row a bit. Barlowe, playing his game, strolled casually behind him. The reporter had a rolling walk, sort of predatory stride. He passed Milo and stopped opposite him.

"You're not making this look much like chance," Milo whispered.

"Shit. Isn't this a bit James Bondy?"

"It's not your job that's on the line . . . You got the money?"

"Like always."

Barlowe fingered his wallet out of his sports coat pocket, held it down close in front of him and slipped out the two twenties and the ten that Evans had given him. He put the wallet back, creased the money and slipped it to Milo. Milo took it, pushed it in his pants pocket.

"The latest," Milo said, "is they're saying it's a cop."

"That's it? I've had that idea myself, remember?"

"No. That's not it. I'm just saying it's a pretty damn steady thought these days."

"All right. What else?"

"They found a button."

Barlowe was quiet a moment. He looked at Milo steadily. "A button?"

"I don't stutter. A button."

"What about a button? What kind of button? What's that got to do with anything?"

"We . . . They think it's off The Hacker's clothes. It's vinyl, like a raincoat button. I've got it in the lab."

"Get anything off the analysis?"

"Not really. Blood. The girl's blood. They know that the killer's blood is type O from the sperm slides taken from both women's bodies."

"They can tell his blood type from sperm?"

"Yeah. Doesn't mean much. Every bozo on the street is damn near O type."

Barlowe rubbed his chin. "A raincoat button, huh?"

"That's right. They're trying to connect it somehow."

"What's the nigger think of all this?"

Milo cringed at the word "nigger." He might be an informer these days, but he thought Hanson was a good cop, a black cop, not a nigger. He didn't say anything to that effect. He just said, "You mean Lieutenant Hanson?"

"Yeah, Lieutenant Hanson."

"I don't know yet. Right now he probably doesn't make anymore of it than I do."

"And what do you make of it, Sergeant Milo?"

"Not much. It's just a button. But I know this much. It wasn't raining the day of the DeMarka murder."

"Interesting," Barlowe said, "damn interesting."

"That's all. That's all I've got for you."

"All right, but listen: I want you to get a copy of the note that came to the paper this morning. You know about that don't you?"

"Hanson and Clark brought it in . . . Why a copy?"

"Doesn't matter why. You get a copy and I slip you another fifty."

Milo licked his lips. "This is all getting warm about the ears, Barlowe."

"All right, sixty bucks, and that's more than it's worth. I can damn near remember the thing word by word. I just need a copy to be safe."

Milo massaged his face nervously with his fingers.

"Well?" Barlowe said.

"Okay. But this is it, the last time."

"You're getting out of the informer business, huh?"

Milo nodded slowly. "At least for awhile. Hanson's really hot on this case."

"You're telling me," Barlowe said. "He damn near slung me around the paper this morning. Big, ugly nigger."

"I wish he had," Milo said flatly.

"Don't wish too much. I might just let slip who my source is to Hanson and your Captain. What's that old bastard's name?"

Milo didn't answer.

"Fredricks, isn't it? Well, Fredricks and Hanson might love to hear about all the nice favors you've been doing me, and about all the nice, green bills I've been slipping you."

"You sonofabitch."

"Exactly. Now you get me that note and whatever else I need."

Milo looked at Barlowe firmly. "The note and that's it. You can do whatever the hell you want to after that. You can't blackmail me. It would get you in as much hot water as I am."

Barlowe smiled. Milo thought the teeth looked predatory sharp. "Very well. We both got each other by the balls. You make this the last one . . . but make it quick. Remember. You've got more to lose than I have. Ain't me with a jellyfish for a kid."

"You sonof . . . " Milo's hand shot out and grabbed Barlowe by the collar. A young woman browsing in the children's section turned to look at them. Her eyes were wide, her lips slack.

"Temper, temper," Barlowe said, and he moved Milo's hand aside. "Very un-James Bond like, very uncool. No use in secret meetings when you draw attention to yourself, Mr. Tough Plain Clothes, Bargaining Detective."

Milo let go of Barlowe.

"That's better," Barlowe said straightening his shirt. He was smiling his sharp-toothed smiled again.

"I'm sorry . . . You shouldn't have said that."

"Yeah," Barlowe said. There didn't seem to be much conviction in his voice. "You're a pretty tough dude, aren't you?"

"Not nearly as tough as Hanson's going to be on the both of us when he finds out, and he just might. He's like a bulldog. Once he locks into something he doesn't let go."

"A tough guy, huh?"

"They don't come any tougher," Milo said.

Barlowe nodded. "So long, Sergeant Milo . . . and get that note to me. Just mail it to the paper . . . I mean if it's good enough for The Hacker it's good enough for you . . . Right?"

Milo didn't answer.

Barlowe turned to walk away.

Milo noticed that the woman in the children's section had moved across the store, but she was still throwing looks his way. Oh the hell with it, he thought.

He turned to watch Barlowe going out the door, making with that odd, predatory stride.

WEDNESDAY . . . 1:25 p.m.

Clark belched.

"Jesus," Hanson said.

"Emily Post doesn't eat at my house," Clark said.

"Or here at the station either, I see."

"Correct. Did you know that in some places, a belch is the polite compliment to a tasty meal."

"You call a pepperoni pizza that tasted like cardboard and leather a culinary delight . . . and cold yet?"

"You still harping about how long it took me?"

"Well, you did just go down to the corner, not all the way to Italy . . . although considering the temperature of the thing, Italy might well be within the realm of reality."

"This act won't get you on the late show. Ain't funny enough . . . didn't you say you had something to tell me after we finished our lovely repast."

"I did."

"Spring it on me."

Hanson pulled the note Warren had written from beneath the edge of his typewriter. "Tell me what you make of this?"

Clark took the note, sipped his Coke and winced. "Too much fuckin' ice in these things, taste like cistern water." He sat the Coke down and read the note.

When he was finished he looked up at Hanson.

"Damn nice of him to go to all that trouble. How come you're suddenly on Warren's hit parade. He's usually about as exciting and concerned as one of his fellow corpses."

Hanson smiled. "He's not that bad. I think these murders have hit a cord with him . . . It's his interest, his secret passion, he told us so himself."

Clark nodded. "A button, huh?"

"Uh huh." Hanson parked his elbows on the desk.

"Why do you think a raincoat button was in the gal's belly?"

"Maybe like Warren said, it could be a nut's reason . . . or

140

maybe . . . "

"Maybe what?"

"Maybe he was wearing the raincoat. That makes more sense."

"No rain that day."

"True," Hanson said slowly.

"You've got a theory. Right?"

"Sort of. The more I think about it the more it grows."

"How about the more you talk about it?" Clark said eagerly.

"All right. Try this on for size."

"I'm listening."

"The guy, The Hacker, was wearing a raincoat even though it wasn't raining that night. Correct?"

"Correct."

"See any sense in that, Joe?"

"Not really . . . Maybe the guy's some kind of fetish nut . . . A flasher even."

"Maybe. But this guy seems to have some kind of sense about what he's doing. I mean he has been careful so far. Wearing a raincoat would be a bit obvious . . . Unless he just puts it on at certain times."

"Just for the murders."

"Yeah."

"So he's got a controlled fetish. So what?"

"No. That isn't what I'm getting at . . . I mean you can't rule out anything with nuts, but I'm saying this guy has a practical side. Think about it."

"The blood!"

"Uh huh."

"Of course. It splatters on the raincoat instead of him."

"That way," Hanson said leaning back in his chair, "he can just slip off the raincoat, wrap it around the murder weapon — sword, bayonet, whatever, and . . . well, in this case, the victim's heart, and presto . . . "

"He's not covered with blood," Clark added.

"A little package under his arm wouldn't draw attention."

"Off he strolls into the night, easy as you please . . . But one thing?"

"Yeah."

"According to the autopsy report, the girl was raped like the last. Raped after death to be exact. Messy business raping a corpse in that kind of condition."

"No problem. The raincoat again. He just unbuttons a couple of buttons, slips out his dick and goes to it."

"Ahhhh. That's how the button came off."

"Yep."

"Sherlock," Clark said. "You outdid yourself."

"Thank you, Watson. Elementary, really."

Clark rubbed his chin. "So all he's got to do is wipe himself off on a sheet or the girl's clothes and he's tidy as a butler. Up comes the pants, off comes the raincoat. He wraps up his gear and gets."

"Yeah. But his days are numbered."

"Another lead?"

"No. Just a promise," Hanson said solemnly.

"Here we go again."

Hanson darted Clark with his eyes. "Yeah, here we go again."

Clark sighed. "Taking this awful damn personal, aren't you?"

"It's always personal with me, Joe. You know that. Usually you too, man. What's wrong?"

"Nothing. Nothing . . . It's just . . . Well, I hate to see you so worked up over this guy. This is more than personal . . . It's an obsession. I'm sort of afraid you'll do something foolish. I don't want to lose you off the force."

"Oh come on."

"Dead serious. You're really wrapped up in this one." Clark smiled thinly. "I mean, hell, man. Now that I'm broke in I'd rather keep working with you. After your training ain't nobody else going to have me anyway."

Hanson was touched. He smiled. "You've got a point there."

"Damn right."

No longer smiling. "But I'm going to get him, Joe. Ain't no way that bastard's going to get away. No way."

"All right. I'll go with that. But let the system handle him. Don't do something foolish."

"You like the way the system handles things, Joe?"

"No. But you can't . . . "

"No buts! That insane bastard is going to be dead if I catch him."

"Lower your voice," Clark said nervously.

"And you know what, Joe?" Hanson said in a lower tone.

"What?"

"Another hunch. I think the bastard just might be a cop."

"You're kiddin'."

"Do I look like I'm kiddin'?"

Clark shook his head.

"It's bad enough that the whole goddamned police force stinks with corruption, but if this guy is a cop, then what? How's that going to look? If he's a cop I want him worse than ever."

"What makes you think a cop?"

"The notes. Right under our cop noses. Remember?"

"Yeah, I remember."

"He's taunting us, telling us consciously or unconsciously."

"Maybe he means it figuratively."

"Maybe. And maybe that's the way he knows what goes on here, how he knows to cover up evidence."

"But why would some guy just suddenly flip out?"

"It happens. Remember Charles Whitman and the U. T. tower?"

Clark nodded. "Okay . . . I can buy that."

"Then can you buy me tellin' you he's a dead sucker?"

"Gorilla, I've worked with you awhile now. This don't sound like you. The tactics you're talking about are not dissimilar to those we're supposed to be against. Like I said before, getting rough now and then, or running a bluff is one thing, but you're talking about cold-blooded murder."

"In this guy's case I can make an exception."

"There should be no exceptions."

"None for cruelty. None for abusing justice. None for personal gain. But for eliminating a cancer from society . . . isn't that what we're here for?"

"Very self-righteous, but it just doesn't wash."

"Doesn't it . . . We are here for justice, correct?"

"Yes, but we're not the judge and the jury."

Hanson shook his head. "That's the way it is, Joe. I'm going to do the world a favor. I promise."

Clark grew silent. He believed Hanson wasn't just blowing. He meant exactly what he said. And that worried him.

6

WEDNESDAY . . . 7:15 p.m.

Rachel's dinner was fine, but Hanson's palate was dead. It all tasted the same to him, bland. He stirred the food on his plate with his fork and said not a word.

Rachel and JoAnna gave each other a look.

JoAnna said, "Daddy, what's the matter?"

Hanson tried to smile. "Not feeling well."

"Again," Rachel said softly.

"Yeah. Again," Hanson said.

"You ought to see a doctor, daddy."

"This is something he can't help with, I'm afraid." Hanson stood up from the table. "Excuse me girls, but I sort of need to be alone." He said the last sentence timidly, as though he were afraid of insulting them.

"It's all right," Rachel said. "I understand."

"Just take a short drive," he said. "Maybe stop off at a magazine rack and look around . . . something . . . just need to clear the head."

"We understand, honey," Rachel said.

Hanson started for the door.

"Daddy," JoAnna said, "I hope you feel better."

"Me too, baby," Hanson said, "me too."

WEDNESDAY . . . 8:15 p.m.

The room was a head, the window was a murky eye.

He stood before the window that looked down into the filthy street. It seemed there was always garbage, no matter how often the garbage men came. Somehow, he found that pleasing.

He opened the window. Up with the lid of the eye.

The city drifted in. It was as if he could smell the women. Out there, waiting for him, not with anticipation, but with fear. Pleasing, that thought, very pleasing.

He placed his hands on the window sill and looked at them. Strong, hard hands; hands sometimes dipped in red. It vaguely reminded him of a quotation.

Who said it? How did it go?

Oh yes . . . Was Aristotle . . . and the quote was, God . . . No. Not God. It was, "Nature has made the hand of man the principal organ and instrument of man's body."

He held up his hands and clenched them in front of his face.

True enough, true enough.

WEDNESDAY . . . 9:45 p.m.

The drive had done him little, if any, good.

Hanson came in quietly, closed the door softly.

"It's all right," Rachel said from the stairs. "I'm still awake."

Hanson looked at her shadowed form sitting at the top of the steps. "Waiting on me?"

"I don't mind." Rachel stood up and came down the staircase. "JoAnna asleep?"

"Finishing up her homework. She made a C in English last time, you know?"

"Yeah, I know," Hanson said dryly. "She could make whatever grades she wanted to."

Rachel came to his arms, they embraced and kissed. When they came apart Rachel said, "What's bothering you, baby? What's wrong?"

"The Hacker. It's eating me up inside . . . I even said some crazy things to Joe today . . . That wasn't the first time."

"You need to get off this case, Marve."

"I can't. I can't do that. No matter what, I can't. I think what I need is to get out of this goddamned job, that's what I think."

"Then you should. You used to enjoy being a cop. It's eating you alive now."

"I got JoAnna's college to worry about."

"There are other jobs. Just a minute." She moved away from him, went upstairs and returned after less than a minute. There was an envelope in her hand. "This came from Zulean today. They're hiring policemen in Tyler. With your experience you could get a job easy."

Hanson sat down on the floor with his back against the door. Rachel sat down beside him. He put his arm around her.

"That's very tempting," Hanson said.

"Then be tempted."

"After this case, I just might."

"Forget it, Marve."

"I can't," he suddenly snapped.

Rachel's features fell.

"I'm sorry," Hanson said. "I didn't mean to yell at you."

"It's all right," she said weakly, and she stood up.

"I am sorry, truly."

"I believe you, Marve. I'm just going to bed. I can't talk any sense into you, so I'm going to bed. Got to go to work tomorrow, remember. You should go to bed, too."

"I'll be up in a little bit."

"Goodnight, Marve."

"Goodnight."

Feeling like a heel, Hanson watched her go. He knew she was hurt even if she wasn't saying so. Nothing beyond repair, nothing a night's sleep wouldn't cure, but his outburst had been stupid. She was only trying to help, only concerned.

All of this has got to stop, got to find that sonofabitch, got to put an end to his insanity . . . But how do you catch a creature like that? A beast-man of night and deceit.

An idea occurred to him. Warren was interested in necrophilia. Said that himself. Maybe . . .

Hanson got up and went to the telephone. He looked at his watch. It was after ten, a little late for an old man who worked all hours, but . . . Hell, he'd try it. He had to. He looked up Warren's number and dialed.

Warren answered on the third ring.

"Did I wake you?" Hanson said.

"No. Who is this?"

"Lieutenant Hanson."

"Oh, Lieutenant. How are you?"

"Fine . . . listen, could you do me a favor?"

"Well, I can try. What's the favor?"

"I need to see you. I want to talk to you about this Hacker guy."

"Me?"

"You said it was your hobby."

"Sure . . . but the psychiatrist . . . "

"Hasn't been worth a hill of beans," Hanson filled in quickly.

"You know I'd be glad to help, Hanson, but I couldn't know anything the psychiatrist doesn't know. I'm a medical examin—"

"You might know something I need. The shrinks are too tied up with their own theories. I just want some straight goods on necrophilia, the nature of it, not some formal doctor's scribbling. I need something that can help me learn how the bastard thinks."

"Very well . . . but tomorrow night after work. Is that all right with you? I mean I could talk to you tomorrow at work, but this might take some time and I've got to saw a lot of brains up tomorrow, run some specimens . . . "

"Not tonight?"

"Oh. Well I don't know . . . Tell you what. I'm going to be up, oh say another hour . . . "

"Fine, I'll come over."

"Wait a minute. Let me finish. I'm going to be up another hour, and in that hour I'll go through some of my books and files, and tomorrow night I'll be ready for you."

Hanson was suddenly assaulted by his impoliteness. "Sure, Doc. I'm sorry. I seem to be running on dinghy fuel here lately."

"Quite all right . . . Now I'll talk to you tomorrow at work, but we might have to compress it all into . . . "

"No. That's fine. Tomorrow night, around eight?"

"Make it seven."

"Good, seven then."

They said their goodbyes and Hanson went up to bed.

7

THURSDAY . . . 9:05 a.m.

"Captain wants to see you."

"All right," Hanson said into the phone. "Thanks."

He hung up and rose from his chair. Clark was snipping out Barlowe's column again this morning, and this time it was blasting the police. He had *The Post* and *The Chronicle* by his chair and he had already stated that even the conservative papers were starting to sound like lurid tabloids where The Hacker was concerned. Hanson didn't quite agree with that, but it was true that the killer, and *The Bugle*, were setting an odd and discomforting tone.

"I'll be back. Think the Captain wants to gnaw my ear for something."

"Uh oh," Clark said.

"Uh oh is right."

Hanson went to the Captain's office.

"Take a chair," Captain Fredricks said. Fredricks was a lean, fiftyish man with a perpetual five o'clock shadow. His jaw looked as if it were made of granite, his nose was a beak. He looked a lot like Dick Tracy with light brown hair.

Hanson sat down uncomfortably in one of the smooth black leather chairs that graced the carpet in front of Fredricks' desk.

Fredricks stood up from his chair, clasped his hands behind his back and walked to the window overlooking the parking lot. Hanson noticed that his dark blue shirt and darker blue slacks looked as if they had just come off the rack. Which they hadn't. Hanson had seen him in that outfit at least a hundred times. Fredricks was always immaculate. His shoes even looked brand new and spit polished. Some people are like that, thought Hanson. His own body seemed to excrete some sort of acid that ate and wrinkled the clothes he wore in less than twenty-four hours. No matter what he wore and how much time he took to get ready, he always had a slept-in look.

Fredricks turned away from the window, kept his arms behind him, rested his hands on the window sill. The overhead light hit his broad maroon and blue striped tie. It appeared to shimmer.

"How long have you been on this police force, Hanson?"

Uh oh, thought Hanson, here it comes. "About twenty years, sir."

"That's a long time."

"Yes, sir . . . Sir?"

Fredricks said, "Yes?"

"You've got something to say, sir, say it. No offense. But that's a line for rookies."

Fredricks smiled. His teeth all looked capped. What made Hanson mad was the fact that he knew they weren't capped. "Sometimes a veteran acts like a rookie."

"I'm wounded to the core," Hanson said dryly.

Fredricks didn't lose his smile. "Very well. You know what this is about?"

"The incident in Evans' office at *The Bugle*."

"Well. It's good to know our actions there aren't so commonplace that you're having a hard time remembering what you're on the carpet for."

"No sir. No problem remembering. I did shoot a couple of pedestrians this morning, but since they weren't in the crosswalk . . ."

"That'll be enough, Lieutenant. I'm convinced you're a wit." Hanson was surprised to note that there still wasn't any anger in Fredricks' voice.

"Evans call this in?"

"It doesn't matter."

"Barlowe?"

"I said, it doesn't matter. Now I'm trying to be lenient with this, so shut up. Got me?"

"Yes sir."

"A man of your age and skill should know better than to perform such an outburst."

"Captain . . ."

157

"I'm not finished. It's bad for the force. It's bad for me, and worse yet, and of more immediate concern to you, it's bad for one Lieutenant Marvin Hanson. Is any of this soaking into your thick skull?"

"Yes sir, but—"

"And when things get bad for me on account of you . . . Well now, guess what? I get rid of you." Fredricks walked over to his desk and sat down. "No roughing up the innocent bystanders, Lieutenant. Remember. We aren't even supposed to be mean to the bad guys anymore. We are to be so squeaky clean and nice it'll make your stomach turn over. You got that, Lieutenant?"

"I do."

"That's good. That's real good. You can go now."

Hanson got up and started for the door.

"One thing, Lieutenant."

Hanson stopped with his hand resting on the doorknob. "I understand you're taking this awful personal. That's bad. Real bad. Another outburst of any kind and you're off the case. Another incident like the one at *The Bugle* and you're off the force. I hope my meaning is clear."

"Crystal clear," Hanson said.

"That's good."

Hanson half opened the door.

"And Lieutenant . . . "

"Yes sir."

"Unofficially, I wish you'd slammed Barlowe one in the mouth and let him digest his teeth."

Hanson smiled.

"You're a good cop," Fredricks said. "Now get out of here."

8

THURSDAY . . . 6:30 p.m.

Hating the light, he drove slowly, wishing night would fall with the suddenness of thought. The night was his security. His blanket of warmth and power. As time went on, the day became more and more of a nuisance. He often wished that during those hours he could do as the movie vampires do, and crawl into a nice, damp, dirt- and death-smelling coffin to sleep. Sleep until night wove its fine dark patterns. And then from that coffin he could rise and hunt.

Cops everywhere or not, he could wait no longer. This coming night he felt he must find a woman to love with his blade. Find her now, follow her into the darkness and deliver her the well-deserved doom that was the only cure for feminine evil.

But first, before tagging tonight's lamb, he had things to do.

THURSDAY . . . 7 p.m.

Milo jerked his head at the sound of the opening door. Joe Clark stood framed in the doorway.

"Frightened me, Joe."

Clark flipped on the lights. "That little desk lamp isn't much to work by. Didn't know they kept it on the Xerox machine these days."

"Yeah . . . Well, I was Xeroxing a little something."

"I see that. Can I have a look?"

"Well . . . Yeah, I guess so."

Clark walked over to the Xerox machine and stood next to Milo. He lifted up the light shield cover, picked up the piece of paper there and turned it over.

"Interesting," Clark said. "An update on our progress with The Hacker."

"A duplicate for the files," Milo said. "Think maybe you should cut that light . . . I mean I don't need all that light for what I'm doing. Conservation and all."

Clark looked at Milo with an expression that said, "Don't make me laugh."

"You're sweating, Milo. Doesn't seem that hot in here to me. Why don't you take off your jacket?"

"That's a good idea." Milo pulled off his sports coat and draped it over the edge of the machine. He watched as Clark took the paper over to the file cabinet.

"Drawer's still unlocked," Clark said. He opened it and thumbed through the folders. His long fingers came to rest on one. He pulled it out and flipped it open. "Well, I'll be damned."

"What's that?" Milo asked a bit too urgently. His eyes darted first to Joe then to the door.

"You're not going to believe this, Milo."

"Believe what?"

"Why there's a copy already in here, just like there's supposed to be."

"That right?"

"Uh huh. One for evidence and one for the morgue file here. Unless special authorization is cleared, that's the exact number that there's supposed to be. Funny how these things get by you, huh, Milo?"

"Funny."

"You want to see? Come take a look."

"No. I'll take your word for it."

"You must be overworking, Milo. Forget a little thing like that." Clark looked at his watch. "Why, Milo. It's way past hours for you."

"Yeah, I guess so. Got sorta wrapped up."

Clark nodded pleasantly. "Well, I'll just slip this back into the file here." Clark did that as he spoke, closed the cabinet drawer, "and you won't have to worry about that sucker. Right?"

"Right. I guess I forgot."

"I guess so. But a copy each, plus a carbon is all you need. And since that was the carbon on the machine. Well, no need to go into that. You're all through for the night. Let's go, Milo."

"Go where?" Milo was sweating B.B.'s now.

"Home, of course. Where else?" Clark smiled broadly.

"You're not . . . "

"Going to turn you in? No. I don't think so. Listen, Milo. We don't need the newspaper working on this case along with us, you know."

"Just a few dollars. That's all I was taking, Joe. I wasn't givin' him much."

"Don't care if it was for free. Let's get out of here before I do turn you in."

"Maybe it's good with the paper printing this stuff and all. Fires us up. Maybe the paper comes up with some new leads and angles."

"Milo," Clark said calmly.

"Yes." Milo's voice was as thin as a communion wafer.

"Shut up. If it wasn't for your kid I'd turn you over so fast it'd make your head swim. I've a big urge just to send you home across your saddle, and believe me, if Gorilla knew you were the one — and I'm sure he suspects since he's no fool — he'd snap you in half like a fortune cookie."

Milo put his coat on.

"Git!" Clark said.

"How'd you know?"

"Why I'm a trained detective, Milo. Hunches, observation. If Gorilla wasn't so rattled these days he'd already have nabbed you. Thank the Lord for his preoccupation. And Milo, you look guilty as hell. You look about as calm these days as a blood-soaked rat in a cage full of hungry cats. In other words — you do not have a poker face. Go!"

"About locking up?"

Clark held out his hand. "Toss me the keys. I'll do it for you."

"It's my job. I'm not supposed to . . . "

"You're kidding. You're not supposed to pass out evidence either."

"But . . . "

"Give me the goddamned keys, Milo, 'cause if you don't, I'm gonna see you in one hell of a fine mess." Clark bobbed his open palm up and down. "Come on. I'll give them back in the morning . . . Maybe. That's if I don't decide to turn you in. Right now I trust my locking up better than yours. I've got a key, but somehow I'll sleep better knowing you don't."

Milo took the keys from his pocket and tossed them to Clark. He said, "Thanks for not saying anything, Joe."

"Isn't for you, Milo. It's for your boy. Now get the hell out. And Milo — if you want to be sneaky, don't act so sneaky. Know why I'm not worried about the light? It's because I went down to Evidence and signed in as soon as I saw you go in here. I signed in to look at The Hacker material."

"I didn't want my name on the register after hours."

"It's more stupid to come in here with your pass key, not signed in and after hours." Clark made a clicking sound with his tongue. "Stupid, Milo. Real stupid. Now go."

Milo went.

When he was gone, Clark began to look through the files on The Hacker again.

THURSDAY . . . 7:05 p.m.

"I'm sorry I'm late," Hanson said.

"Just five minutes," Doc Warren said opening the door wider. "Come in, come in."

Warren's house was warm and comfortable looking. The furniture was expensive, but it didn't have a show room look. The place looked lived in.

"I hope this little appointment isn't disturbing anything," Hanson said.

"Not at all, Lieutenant, not at all. I live alone and company's nice for a change. Haven't had much of that since Juanita died."

"Sorry."

"Quite all right. Been three years now. Come, this way into

the study. I've marked a few things that might interest you."

"Thank you . . . And call me Marvin or Hanson, but not Lieutenant."

"Very well, Marvin." Warren opened a door before them, held it to allow Hanson to enter first. It was a room full of books. The carpet was rust colored and matched well with the redwood bookshelves. There was a large desk in front of a window at one end, an old, battered typing chair drawn up before it, and in the middle of the room was a huge wire spool that had been turned into a table. Two comfortable and fairly worn chairs were drawn up to it. The spool was littered with old moisture rings from glasses and bottles. An ashtray full of ash and cigar butts was on the table.

"Juanita gave me this room to do as I pleased," Warren said. "I pleased to keep it a mess. Pardon the old furniture."

"Not at all," Hanson said. "I like the hell out of it. I have a den, not private, but it's a place to relax. This looks like a hell of a fine place to relax."

"Sit down . . . Or look at the books . . . You a book man, Marvin?"

"Very."

"Good. That's good. A man that loves books — or a woman — is the salt of the earth. If they don't love books then they aren't worth knowing." Warren smiled. "You may quote me on that. I'm getting so I babble."

Hanson smiled. "I'll look at the books."

"Good, good. Right back . . . Miller beer okay?"

"Wouldn't have any other if I had a choice."

167

"All the better." Warren went out and closed the door.

Hanson walked down the rows of books. They went from a shelf height of six-feet to floor level. The majority of the books were on crime, violent crime. There were also a few novels by Hemingway, Faulkner, and Fitzgerald. There was a six-foot-long shelf full of Eighty-seventh Precinct mysteries.

"Ah, good man," Hanson said aloud as his eyes came to rest on a favorite of his, Raymond Chandler's *The Big Sleep*, and here was John Ball's *In the Heat of the Night*. He took that one down and flipped it open.

The door opened and Warren came in with the beers, both held in one hand between fingers. He walked over to Hanson, looked at the book he held, handed the detective a beer. "Ball," he said. "I like his stuff."

"Me too," Hanson said. "This book especially. It seems a bit more hardboiled than the later ones in the series."

"Agreed," Warren said. "The character changes a bit, becomes more Sherlockian. But I like that too. I think he might have been trying for a more serious tone in the first one."

Hanson slipped the book back into place, then twisted the top off his beer.

"Let's sit," Warren said. "Cigar?"

"That would be nice," Hanson said. Hanson sat down in one of the comfortable chairs, put his beer on the spool table.

Warren set his down and went over to his desk. He came back with a few books under his arm and a box full of cigars. "Not the most expensive cigars in the world, certainly they're not the kind you roll around in your fingers next to your ear and listen for the crispness, but they're tasty and smoke good."

"I used to smoke grapevines, so what do I know about cigars. They're tobacco. That's enough. I like one occasionally."

Warren set the books on the table, lifted the lid on the cigar box, selected two long, brown cigars. He gave Hanson one and himself one. He took a book of matches from the corner of the cigar box and once the detective had the cigar unwrapped and in his mouth, lit Hanson's. He lit his own with the same match.

"Now," Warren said, "let's get down to business."

"Tell me about this guy, about necrophilia."

Warren swigged his beer, puffed his cigar, then pursed his lips. After a moment of thought he repeated the performance, one, two, three. Then: "Well, Marvin. I think this guy is more than a necrophiliac. If what he said in his note about frying the breast is true, he shows cannibalistic tendencies as well. Not to mention a horde of other symptoms. His is the most exaggerated form of necrophilia. You see, the real purpose behind necrophilous killers is not to kill, but to dismember the body. Of course, to do that the victim must die. With this killer, however, I feel he is an odd and uncomfortable mixture of necrophiliac and sadist. He enjoys his crimes. He taunts the police with notes. He writes the newspapers. This man is no fool, he's sick, sick, sick . . . You're frowning . . . "

"Sorry. Just to me sickness means something else. I don't want to help the guy . . . I want to catch him, not because he's sick, but because he's a coldblooded murderer."

"I understand fully," Warren said. "Another beer?"

"No. Go on."

"I'd say this man is one that has recently gone over the edge."

"Someone that has carried these urges with him for a long time?" Hanson asked.

"Correct. He . . . right off let me say I'm not a psychiatrist and don't claim knowledge in that area . . . but he may well be a split personality. That sort of thing doesn't happen as often as you think. The movies and books we read sometimes lead us to believe otherwise, but it's just not true. It does happen occasionally however, and this just might be a classic case. If he is a split personality, a true split, he may not even be aware of what he does when he's not The Hacker. He could be anybody. You. Me."

"Not me. This guy's white."

Warren leaned back in his chair and smoked his cigar. "Oh."

"The greasepaint we found. His references to niggers in his notes. A black man wouldn't need a greasepaint disguise, and we feel certain that's what that was, and he wouldn't refer to his own kind as niggers . . . not likely anyway, least not in the context of the notes."

"I don't know," Warren said. "You see, if this guy is a true split personality, he might well be a black man with a separate white existence."

"Come again."

"Well. When he's the murderer, he might think of himself as white. He might have rubbed grease paint on a black face and not even be aware that he's already black. Even if he looked in a mirror

170

he would see a white face if that is the identity he was living at the moment. It may even be some deep dark racial conflict that sent him over the edge."

"Jesus."

"I said he could be a split personality. Not that he was. Most likely, considering the few true cases, he's not. He's calculating, intelligent and resourceful. He could have been carrying this around with him for years. One day he just couldn't hold it back anymore, and presto, The Houston Hacker is born."

"I think maybe it's a cop."

Warren nodded his head. "Possible. Or maybe someone connected with the cops indirectly."

"I think he's right out of the department. He seems to know our every move."

"It's a thought," Warren said.

"This necrophilia stuff," Hanson asked, "is it common?"

"More common than you think. All abnormalities spring out of normalities."

"Come again. That's a little heavy for me."

"I mean we all have tendencies for such things . . . even necrophilia. You and I are excellent examples. We're in jobs that deal with death, and I, of course, work bodies over in the same way The Hacker does, but for other reasons. You see death constantly. Perhaps you and I have a bit stronger necrophiliac tendencies than most, or otherwise we'd be in a different business. People that gather around car wrecks, that's a mild example. Basically, an attraction to dead things or items dealing with death: coffins, graveyards, that sort of thing. Perhaps even sexual excitement induced by a dead body."

"But . . . " Warren didn't hear him. He was wrapped up in his thoughts, his presentation.

" . . . common enough. Take the example from this book," Warren picked up *On the Nightmare* by Ernest Jones. "It mentions the case of Periander, the Corinthian tyrant who murdered his wife, Melissa, and had sexual intercourse with the corpse." Warren put the book down. The cigar between his fingers was dead. "And then there's the Biblical Herod who was said to have slept with his wife's body for quite some time after she died. This is more than bereavement, this is necrophiliac character. Take Faulkner's short story, 'A Rose For Emily,' more of the same."

"Then these crimes, though not necessarily performed for the intent of murder, are sexual."

"These crimes, unlike most necrophilous intentions that result in the death of the victim, are performed for the satisfaction of both sadistic lust and necrophilous desire. They are definitely sexual in nature, born out of some sort of sexual frustration. And not just the old classic school of can't get any, or can't get it up. It's more than that. Deeper. Much deeper. The problem with this man may well date back to childhood, if I may indulge in a bit of backyard Freud. It has finally boiled to the surface."

"And he'll kill and kill and kill."

"Unless it satiates itself. Dies within."

"You mean he could just quit?"

"It's not an accepted thought, and not likely, I admit, but

possible. Or so I think."

"He could just stop all of this? Blend back in?"

"I'm saying it's possible. Jack the Ripper may well have done just that. There are a number of theories concerning the Whitechapel murders, none any better than another. Some think that a man found drowned with stones in his pocket, Druitt," Warren picked from the books on the table *The Complete Jack the Ripper* and shook it, "I believe was his name, might have been the ripper, and that with his death, suicide, or perhaps execution performed by his family who were aware of his nocturnal prowlings, the murders came to an end. Of course there are other suspects. Some say he may have migrated to America. I think he just stopped. This necrophilous appetite manifested itself, he satisfied it and it died, at least temporarily. Perhaps he surfaced again later, performed more crimes. But what I'm saying is that perhaps this odd ball character, to put it mildly, comes in waves. Maybe it only washes to shore once, fills the already frustrated necrophiliac with overwhelming urges, which he performs, and away it goes, low tide, never to roll in again."

"That's rather contrary to what's thought by most, isn't it?"

"It is. I told you I wasn't a psychologist or a psychiatrist, just an interested party. Very interested."

"Thank you. You've been a great help. Now for the last and most important question. How can I find this man? What would he be like?"

"Like you or me. He could have a family . . . "

"A family?"

"Think of the infamous Boston Strangler, if they have the right person. He was a good family man. Wife and children . . . Part-time murderer. I'd say chances are, however, that our man doesn't have a family. Maybe he once did. Perhaps this is part of his grief, or that little something that has given his compulsion fuel. He's probably a lonely man. Perfectly normal man on the outside, but inside . . . turmoil. Good chance that he lives in a section of town that's rundown. This would be in keeping with his necrophilous character. It would help to control his impulses. He might even have a job with garbage, sewer . . . the morgue. Anything that contains putrid odors, as this is often an attraction. Maybe the place where he lives is near something like a graveyard, a funeral home . . . Or if he's a split personality, perhaps he goes home to his family, and then, by means of some excuse, perhaps not conscious, he leaves them and goes to another home, the one more in character with his *other* personality."

"He could be living a secret life?"

"Correct. And not even be aware of it. When he's with his family he's John Doe, good husband and father. When he's the other, and in the abode of the other . . . Well, he wouldn't even be aware of his normal existence. If he's a split personality."

"The ghetto might be a place to look."

"Uh huh. But what are you going to do. Knock on doors, say, pardon me is this the residence of The Hacker?"

"I don't know. I'm still holding to that idea about a cop. Matter of fact, something you said tonight worries me a bit. Reminds me of something."

"What's that?"

"You'll excuse me for not saying just now, I hope. I mean it is just a thought and I don't want to go off half cocked. As a matter of fact it bothers me that I'm even thinking it."

"I understand."

Hanson put the remaining portion of his cigar out in the ashtray with a smash and a twist, stood up and held out his hand. Warren took it. They shook. "Thank you," Hanson said.

"By all means. And do come back. I'm pretty lonely sometimes. The wife gone and all, nothing but my work. But I'm not squawking. I like my job . . . Still."

"I understand. And I will come back. See you at work."

"Over another body I presume."

Hanson smiled thinly. "Most likely."

"Come, let me show you out."

On the way out Warren said, "Marvin, remember. The man is sick."

"I'll try to remember that."

"It's in all of us, each and every one of us."

"But only the weak ones become the crazies, The Hacker."

"It has nothing to do with weakness," Warren said.

"My theory. I think it does. Like always, the weak, at least in a case like this where the beast is a detriment to society, should be weeded out."

"It could be anybody, Marvin. If he's a split, it could be you."

Hanson didn't say anything.

"We all have that character of necrophilia deep within us. One of those books I had in there, *A History of Torture and Death,* shows the atrocities that we did in the name of justice and vengeance. They were more often worse than the original crimes. Man is a bloody animal."

"Was. We have laws now."

"Man is the same as always, Marvin."

"I'm sorry. I can't accept that. If there's no order then there's no purpose. I'd as soon not get up in the morning."

"Very well," Warren said leaning his hand against the door sill. "But remember, if you catch him . . . "

"When," Hanson interrupted, "when."

Warren smiled. "When . . . Try to remember that he is a human being."

"It'll be hard," Hanson admitted.

"Try. Promise me you'll try."

"All right, then," Hanson said slowly. "I promise to try." Hanson thought, didn't I make this promise to someone else recently?

"Thank you," Warren said.

"And thank you again for your time."

"I don't think I've been much help."

"Maybe you have. Maybe a lot more than you think. It's got me thinking. That's something. It's made me move a few trees so I can see the forest."

"I hope so."

"Goodnight."

"Goodnight, Marvin."

When Hanson was almost to his car Warren called after him. "And be careful, Marvin. Be careful."

Hanson turned. "I will."

Warren thought, but didn't say, "You better."

Hanson climbed in his car, started it up, turned on the lights and drove away.

Warren watched until Hanson's car was out of sight.

THURSDAY . . . SAME TIME 7:05 p.m.

Herman Park was bathed in comfortable darkness. Milo enjoyed the dark as much as the babe enjoys the womb. It was soothing and gave him time to think. In the background a late night symphony was entertaining an open air audience, and closer to him came the nocturnal prowlings of the zoo animals, roaring and moaning out for a lost world and a freedom most of them had never known. Milo thought if they were free they wouldn't even know what to do with it. He felt equally caged, not by bars but by his inability to live up to the code he had so cherished early in life. Honesty had flown out the window. He rationalized now. Always a good reason for this, a good reason for that. And he couldn't even stand by his word. He had told Barlowe no more, but when that long green danced beneath his nose his word had been weaker than an Egyptian mummy's shroud. Characterless, that's what I am. Characterless.

Out of the shadows at the end of the trail that terminated at his park bench, Milo saw a human form move his way. The roll to the walk was enough to give the man away had he been trying to hide himself. Which he wasn't. Milo looked at his watch. They had planned on 7:15; Barlowe, as usual, was on time.

Barlowe had his hands in his jean pockets, and the tee-shirt he was wearing, an army-green affair, surprised Milo by revealing Barlowe as stoutly built. Somehow, he had always assumed that the man was a wimp.

"Anything for me," Barlowe said taking a seat next to Milo on the bench.

"They caught me, or rather Joe Clark did."

"The nigger's partner?"

"Come on, will you?"

"It's not like they're your buddies."

"They're cops, just like me. Only difference," Milo snarled, "is that I'm dirty and they're not."

"For all you know."

"No. They're not. I know."

"You in hot water?"

"Maybe. Clark let me go. He said he wouldn't tell."

"Then you didn't get a thing for me?"

Milo turned to look at Barlowe full in the face. "I was caught, fuckhead. I told you that. I was lucky to get out with my head. I hate myself enough for going back on my word before. I said no more last time."

"All right. You were caught. He didn't turn you in. You're home free. You lay low for awhile, and then when they figure you've quit, well, you start back. The money will keep coming."

"No it won't."

"My editor— "

"That's not what I mean. I don't want your money. Go wipe your ass on it. I'm through."

"I just might send the cops a little note expressing my appreciation for all you've done."

Milo grabbed Barlowe's tee-shirt. "Go ahead."

"I'm going to let you let go of that shirt all by yourself. 'Cause if you don't I'm going to help you."

"You don't scare me, Barlowe. Here take your shirt." Milo released him and stood up. "You write your little note, fuckhead. See if I care. I'm through. Nothing more from me."

"You're safe, Milo. I was trying to get that extra inch."

Milo shook his head. "Push just as far as you can don't you?"

"That's right," Barlowe said draping his arms over the back of the park bench. "Just as far as I can. That's part of being a reporter. I'm good at it."

"You certainly are."

"I wouldn't report you because it might dry up the rest of my sources if I got to be known as a louse."

179

"I don't think you have to advertise about being a louse, Barlowe. Folks recognize it right off."

"So be it."

Milo turned and started down the dark trail.

Barlowe yelled to him, "Give my regards to your kid, Jello."

Milo trembled, thought, no, he's baiting me. I'm through with him all the way. He kept walking toward the glow of the street lights.

THURSDAY . . . 8 p.m.

Before heading for home he cruised for a victim down Astro-dome way. Passing that landmark monstrosity, it made him think of a huge breast. Now one that size would be fun. It would take forever to carve it into slabs of red, wet meat. An eternity of fun.

A blue '68 Mustang convertible went by him on the right hand side. Long brown hair whipped up into the night wind. The street lights, bright as day, danced off her naked back. She was wearing a bathing suit top, dark green in color. He wondered what she was wearing below. Bathing suit bottoms? Shorts? Jeans? He would soon know.

She took an off ramp.

He moved quickly to the right lane, and at a bit too accelerated a speed, he took the off ramp behind her.

PART THREE:
THE END OF IT ALL

Vengeance is without foresight.
— *Napoleon I*

Justice is truth in action.
— *Joubert*

Self-defense is a virtue, sole bulwark of all right.
— *Byron*

No man ever did a designed injury to another without doing a greater to himself.
— *Henry Home*

"I think there are certain crimes which the law cannot touch, and which therefore, to some extent, justify private revenge."
— *Sherlock Holmes*

1

THURSDAY . . . 8 p.m.

Patricia Quentin had no idea she was being followed.

The day had been one of perfection for her. The lake had been like a giant blue liniment for her bruised and battered soul. She no longer hated Roger, not at all, and by the same token, she knew she no longer loved him. It was as if this day was the punctuation mark that ended her pain.

Just like my Old Man told me, she thought. "Roger's no good. Not worth a dried cow turd." True enough.

I have a new life before me now. As the saying goes: "Today is the first day of the rest of your life."

Wrapped in the joys of emotional freedom, Patricia didn't notice that the same car had been following her for miles, holding back approximately three car lengths. When she reached the residential street where she lived, she was aware of lights hard on the tail of her Mustang, but she wasn't frightened. Not yet.

Driving a bit faster than she cared to, she whipped into her driveway to avoid the car up her tailpipe, and killed the engine. She sat for a moment with her arm thrown back over the seat watching the car that had been behind her.

She was curious, nothing more.

The car went past. She didn't recognize it.

It didn't frighten her when it slowed down at the end of the block and hesitated longer than it needed at the *Stop* sign, then with a sudden spurge, turned right and speeded off. For a moment she thought it might be Roger, drunk again, back to try and satisfy his lust and slash her feelings with his cutting remarks. But if so, he had backed out at the last moment and gone his way.

She got out of the Mustang and closed the door. She wore only a bathing suit. A sharp stone went into the ball of her bare foot, and this demanded her attention. Using one hand to support herself against the hood of the Mustang, she used the other to pluck the rock from her foot.

Headlights bobbed at the far corner of the block, slit the street wide open with light.

Could he have circled? Patricia wondered.

The car was moving slowly, halfway up the block now.

To hell with him, she thought. If it's Roger I'll give him the quick brush off. From now on he's like so much air to me.

Patricia squeezed out a drop of blood from the wound, made a sound like "yetch." Patricia had a weak stomach and hated the sight of blood, especially her own.

Own fault, she thought, locking up your sandals with your towel and tanning lotion. What good are sandals in the trunk?

Her thoughts were interrupted by the sound of a car door closing.

Thinking it was Roger after all, she placed her injured foot on the ground and turned angrily. By God, she'd had it. This was the showdown . . .

The man from the car wasn't Roger. He was coming across the lawn toward her. The car at the curb was most certainly the one that had been tailgating her. Still she didn't recognize it. She kept thinking it would come to her.

The man was halfway across the lawn now. The shadows clung to him like leeches.

An odd and unaccountable tentacle of fear reached into her brain. "Can I help you?" she asked, immediately wishing the words hadn't come out of her mouth. That was what she said at work when people came into the shoe department. Worse yet, her voice had trembled.

"Yes," the man's voice was pleasant enough, dry and husky but certainly not sinister. He was smiling. Against the night the teeth were as white as alabaster. "I'm afraid I'm lost," the man continued. "Not my neighborhood at all. I have a friend name of Gaston lives over this way. You know them? Has a wife, Jean, a little girl named Alice."

"No. I don't believe they live around here."

The man was almost to her.

"Oh, I'm certain it's around here somewhere. I mean I may not know this area, least not immediately, but this is the right end of Houston."

"No one by that name around here," Patricia said. She could see now that the package beneath his arm was not a package at all. It was a bundled up raincoat. It seemed like an odd thing for a man to carry on a perfectly clear, warm night.

The man was an arm's length away now.

"Stop right there," came out of Patricia's mouth before she could prevent it.

The man stopped, put a puzzled look on his face. "Sure."

Suddenly he moved . . . and was on her. His left hand grasped her throat, his right clamped down over her mouth.

Patricia tried to scream but couldn't.

The raincoat had fallen from beneath the man's arm and struck the driveway with a clank. Out of the corner of her eye the struggling Patricia could see something had partially fallen from the folds of the raincoat. Something that glimmered. Something metal. Something sharp.

Patricia kicked the man in the shins. Hard.

He made a pained sound, jerked the hand from her throat and brought it back into her face as a fist.

She kicked once more, weakly this time.

The fist came back again; then it was gone, then back again. Red, white and black flashed alternately before her eyes before flashing together in a pinwheel of color . . . then she fell into unconsciousness. Her last thought before the plunge was that something warm and wet had fallen on her face.

Her eyes, while alert, had been big — big blue china plates of fear. He had enjoyed that immensely. Now the moon and the smog-ridden stars and the street lights shone in her suddenly less wide eyes with a dull, flat glare.

He looked about him quickly. Saw no one.

He dragged her to the house, propped her against the door. He went back to reclaim the raincoat and bayonet. He picked up her ring of keys from where she had dropped them, went back and unlocked the door. Patricia fell back against the floor with a thud.

Taking a firm grip on her thick hair, he pulled her inside and closed the door.

He put the raincoat aside, bent over her and grasped the bottom of her bathing suit, tugged it off in one quick move. Ripping the bathing suit top apart with a frenzied jerk, he stood for a moment basking in her nakedness. Blood was running in slow rivulets from her mouth and nose, branching out at her neck and chin, rolling toward the floor.

He kicked off his shoes, hastily began removing his trousers, so hastily in fact that he ripped his zipper free of the lining. With his pants in a heap on the floor, he pulled on the raincoat, not bothering to remove his shirt. He was much too anxious for a delay.

Any moment someone might show up, a roommate or parent, even. He was certain, because the house had been dark and her car was the only one in the drive, that she was alone. At least for now.

He pulled her legs apart and arranged his penis between the folds of the raincoat. Dropping to his knees between her legs, he watched, mesmerized, as the blood on her face began to widen on her cheeks. Pure beauty.

For a brief moment he felt foolish. Perhaps someone was in the house. Maybe his caution was out the window, a servant to his lust. Certainly this had been a random strike. No careful planning here . . . But the thought melted. He stretched out on top of her and mounted her with a grunt.

He reached the bayonet to him, placed it against her throat, rested both palms on top of the flat side, watched as her eyes tried to draw consciousness to them.

Patricia was aware of pain between her legs and all over her face. Suddenly her vision cleared and she looked up into the eyes of Satan, aware only that something cold was against her throat. She wanted to scream, but only a gurgle came out.

He began the moment he thought she was aware, pressing gently at first.

Beads of blood, like cheap ruby-red costume jewelry, formed at her throat; then her entire neck was a slash of crimson. Her mouth was opening wordlessly. Her eyes were like big china blue plates again.

Timing it simultaneously with the thrust of his hips, he pushed the blade down with all his might.

Her neck exploded in a fountain of red. Blasted his face, the carpet, the walls. The torso, the head hanging to it by only a shred of flesh and bone, began to twist and lurch convulsively.

As the spasms jerked their last he climaxed with a groan. Then, as he lay atop the body bathed in ecstasy, he began to lap the blood from the stump of her neck with a frenzied tongue.

2

FRIDAY . . . 6 p.m.

When he got home from work, the first thing he did was take the head and hand out of the freezer compartment of his refrigerator. He somewhat regretted not keeping the other hand, but he had other plans for it, and wasteful as it seemed at the moment, he was sure it would have the desired effect he wanted. He dismissed that. He would think no more of the other hand. He had the left one and the head.

He took the head and hand, wrapped and frozen inside separate plastic bags, and placed them in the sink. He was about to run warm water over them for thawing when he suddenly hesitated. He took the bag containing the woman's head from the sink, and brushing away the frost with his palm, looked long and hard at it.

The eyes were like cracked blue marbles seen through a thin film of milky water. Lovely now in a different way. And the blood . . . he was glad he hadn't washed it off. It had frozen into lovely patterns. It swept out of her nostrils in rust colored rivers of ice. Her mouth was sealed with it; a red-brown plug of silence.

It was almost a pity to thaw it.

He returned the head to the sink, turned the hot water on it. While the water ran, he got down his cookbook. So far the recipes for pork had worked fine for human flesh; therefore, he saw no reason to deviate.

3

SATURDAY . . . 7:45 p.m.

Rachel was worried about Marvin. At first she thought it was overwork, but as time went on he became worse. More sullen. More withdrawn. It was almost as if there were two of him. One, the man she loved; the other, a remote and nervous soul. And that other was slowly devouring the one she loved.

He had taken to erratic habits. Before, he'd been content to read in his library, or watch an occasional television show, or take her out to eat or to the movies. Now he avoided these things. He came home, preferred to be alone, and then at odd moments would become restless and leave.

"Going down to the drugstore for a magazine," he would say. But he never came back with magazines.

"Going to get a chocolate bar, or something," he would say.

But if anything, he was losing weight, not gaining. He hardly touched his food at home.

As for sex. He hardly seemed aware of her. The bed was for sleeping, nothing more — when he came to bed. Often she would awake and not find him there. He had still not come upstairs. And when he did come to bed she was seldom, if ever, aware of it. She knew he was getting less than three hours of sleep a night. He just sat below in the den and worried, and it was all since this Hacker stuff.

Even now he was gone, had been for an hour and a half.

"I'm going to drive around a bit," he said. "Don't fix supper for me. I'll be back late. Might drop by and see Warren." And then with a look of pain in his eyes, "I've just got to do something. Can't sit. It eats at me if I do." Suddenly he was gone.

At first she thought it might be another woman, but no, she knew him too well for that. Or at least she thought she did . . .

"Mamma?"

Rachel stood at the sink with her arms in dishwashing suds up to the elbow. "Oh . . . I'm sorry, baby. Have you been standing there long?"

"No longer than a couple of weeks. I've been calling you."

Rachel took her hands from the water, shook off the suds, dried them on a hand towel. "What is it, JoAnna?"

"How do I look?"

Rachel surveyed the tight green bell bottoms, the ruffled, white blouse with the low-cut front. "Maybe," Rachel said, "you look a little too good. Know what I mean?"

"Sexy?" JoAnna said with a grin.

"I guess so. I don't think I like you looking sexy."

"You don't exactly dress like Little Black Sambo yourself."

Rachel laughed. "When's Tommy coming by?"

"Eight."

"Where you going tonight?"

"Movie."

"Do I have to ask which one?"

"No. You don't have to check on me like a little girl, though."

"You are a little girl, little girl."

"The Redland."

"A drive-in?"

"Last time I looked."

"Daddy doesn't like you going to drive-ins."

"Afraid I'll get sick from the draft."

"Don't get smart," Rachel said, but she could hardly help smiling. "As long as you stay well dressed you won't get sick . . . about nine months later. Know what I mean?"

"Oh, Mamma. You know me better than that."

Rachel leaned against the cabinet. "Baby. I don't know anybody better than that. At least at an in-door theater you have to consider modesty."

"Mother!"

"Daughter!"

JoAnna frowned. "All right. I'll tell Tommy to forget the drive-in."

Rachel made a motion like a bow being drawn across a violin, made a sad whining noise to go with it.

"Ha, ha," JoAnna said.

The doorbell rang.

"I'll get it, Mamma."

"Probably for you anyway."

Rachel turned back to her dishes. Listened as JoAnna opened the door. Tommy's voice floated back to her. "Man, you're looking good."

"I know it," JoAnna said half giggly.

"You ready?" Tommy asked.

"Yeah. But . . . there's been a change in plans."

"Oh."

Almost whisper soft. "Mamma says no drive-in on account of you know what."

"Oh."

Rachel found herself straining to hear.

Suddenly both JoAnna and Tommy were in the kitchen. "We're going now."

Rachel turned to look at Tommy. He was a tall, handsome boy, almost as dark as Hanson, but not quite. He had a natural hairdo, but not a full-blown one. It was actually rather short. She agreed with JoAnna's choice. He was handsome, and for that matter, nice.

"You look nice yourself, dishsuds and all," Tommy said. "I mean, I was telling JoAnna she looked nice, but if you're any indication of what she's going to look like when she gets older, I think I'll stick around."

And intelligent, Rachel concluded in a half amused way.

"You two be careful and have fun," Rachel said.

"We will," Tommy said. Rachel thought that a bit too certain a statement, and she thought, but didn't say, "What kind of fun?" Nope, she concluded, I'm being an old hen. JoAnna has to make her own mistakes. I can't make them for her or keep her from them. But, on the other hand, I can try.

"Bye, Mom," JoAnna said, kissing Rachel on the cheek.

"Bye, baby. Be careful."

"I'll take care of her," Tommy said. "See you later, Mrs. Hanson. Say hello to Mr. Hanson."

"I will."

JoAnna took Tommy's hand and they started out. They do make a good pair, thought Rachel, as she turned back to her dishes.

Hanson was getting too close. Too damn persistent. But maybe a little direct close-to-home action would make him pull back on the leash. With that in mind, he had planned tonight's events carefully. A little research had turned up the nigger's address and the fact that he had a wife and daughter. Nothing like losing someone you loved to throw a scare into you and hurt you the deepest. Tonight Hanson would hurt to the core.

The van he was using for the job had been candy to steal. He had had to leave his car in a parking lot again and do a bit more walking than he intended, but when he found the van, bright blue with great long yellow flame licks painted on the sides, he felt certain he had a winner. And when he found a key on his special ring that fit the ignition, and when that motor had roared, causing the whole machine to shake eagerly beneath him, he knew his instinct and judgement had been perfect. The van was souped up from the word go.

He now sat at the corner of Hanson's street, watching, observing. He had been there for fifteen minutes, just long enough to see a sleek black Grand Prix drive up in Hanson's drive, and observe a black youth get out and go inside. Almost absently, he fondled the raincoat that lay on the floor between the van's bucket seats, felt the hard metal of the bayonet through the vinyl. Feeling it was as comfortable as feeling his penis, rubbing it erect. In fact, caressing the bayonet was bringing him to erection. He would satisfy that need shortly, but for now, he must wait.

He was eager to deliver the box, although in some ways, he thought using the contents this way was wasteful. He had intended to mail it, but no, this method was far more interesting . . . dramatic even.

The front door of the Hanson residence opened again. This time the teenager came out with an attractive young girl. He watched her through narrowed eyes, observed the sensual movements of her hips. Soft brown love on a cushion of blood.

She was the one, he decided.

He watched as the youth backed the Grand Prix out of the drive. They did not come in his direction. The Grand Prix moved slowly to the block's end and took a right.

Counting to ten slowly, he started up the van and drove away from the curb.

The box would have to wait.

He followed them out Southmore, watched as they turned into a theater parking lot. Pulling in after them, he parked some distance from their chosen space and watched. They got out of the Grand Prix and walked up to the theater, arm in arm, laughing together.

There were two long lines for the twin cinema. One of the movies was *Prophecy*; the other *Love at First Bite*. They fell into the line for the latter.

His watch showed 8:27. Movie must begin at 8:30, thereabouts. Counting previews of coming attractions, snack bar advertisements and the movie, they would be in there for at least two hours. If he knew youngsters like he thought, they would have plans after the movie, and not just for a Coke. When he was growing up they sometimes called it "going to the woods," "grubbing," or "parking." Whatever, it was popular then and would be now. He wished he hadn't missed out on that fun, but perhaps tonight he could make up for vacant youthful memories.

He checked his watch one more time, started up the van and headed back to the Hanson residence.

After the dishes, Rachel decided to treat herself to a small glass of wine. She had just poured it and settled down at the dining room table when the doorbell rang.

Never fails, she thought, never fails.

She went to the door, checked through the peep-hole. No one. That struck her as odd. Too odd. Kids playing pranks, perhaps. Perhaps. She went to the window, eased back the curtain and peeped out. There was no one standing at the door, but there was something before it. A box. Peripherally she saw lights, turned to look.

A blue van was pulling quickly away from the curb.

Odd, she thought.

She waited five more minutes, then went to the door and picked up the box. HANSON was marked on top of it in big, magic marker letters. Sort of late for a delivery. But considering there were no stamps, hardly a professional presentation anyway.

She turned the box around and upside down. Something heavy clunked inside.

Curious.

She closed the door and set the box on the dining room table, finished her wine. It was addressed HANSON, and although that was her name too, and she could open the box herself, she was certain it was addressed to Marve since that was what he most often went by. Usually with a great big "Mr." in front of it.

She'd wait until he got home.

Unless he took too long, and then her curiosity was bound to get the better of her.

Still nearly an hour and a half to waste. He knew just how to do it.

Rachel was just about to open the package when she heard a car in the drive. She went to the window and looked out. It was Hanson. Her intentions had been to confront him as soon as he arrived, try to get to the bottom of his recent insanity. Late night drives, disorientation. She wanted to talk to him again about giving up the big city, moving out to his grandpa's farm. But the minute she saw him, saw the odd look on his face — a poor mask for internal frustration — she decided to let it ride.

She met him at the door like a happy puppy.

"Well," he said when she opened the door, "you certainly look happy."

"And why not. We — or maybe you — have a secret admirer."

Hanson came inside. "A secret admirer?"

"Someone who lusts for you at a distance. Someone with a warm spot in their heart — or elsewhere — for your big, masculine body."

Hanson smiled. "Okay. What's up?"

She took him by the hand. "Follow and all shall be revealed."

She led him to the dining room, pointed to the box on the table. "Someone rang the doorbell, took off and left the box there. It has *Hanson* written on the top, so I assume it's for you. And if you don't open it immediately I'm going to break your arm off at the elbow. I've been dying to look at it."

"Who's it from?"

"A secret admirer, I told you. Just *Hanson* on the box, nothing else. No return address. In fact, it wasn't delivered by post."

"Huuummm."

"Come on, you big dummy. Open it."

"All right, all right."

Hanson picked up the box and started for the den.

"Hey," Rachel called, "where you going?"

"Come on. I'm going to open it in the den where I can sit in my chair."

"Now that's rich. Yassa Massa, I'll sit at you feets while you opens it, and maybe kind massa you'll let me have a peek."

"Maybe," Hanson said. He went into the den, Rachel hot on his big heels.

Hanson sat down in "his" chair, set the box in his lap, cranked a cigar out of his shirt pocket, and carefully plucking a match from the gopher pack he carried, struck it and lit his cigar, puffing slowly.

"Quit stalling, you big ape."

"Ehh, ehh, ehh. My secret admirer."

"Well the admired is going to have a big hole in his head from my fist if he doesn't open the package."

"Hold on to your horses."

Hanson edged himself sideways in the chair and dug out his pocket knife, settled back comfortably and opened the smaller, sharper blade. He cut at the paper tape that held the lid in place. When it was sliced free, he folded the blade in and returned the knife to his pocket. He set the box on the floor in front of his chair.

"Come on, come on," Rachel said, as excited as a kid at Christmas.

He peeled back the cardboard flaps. Inside was a folded sheet of paper and a plastic bag.

The smell hit him first.

"Get back, Rachel."

"What? I want to—"

"Trust me, baby. Get back."

Rachel stood up, moved across the room to the sofa and sat down.

There was a hand inside the bag.

A woman's hand, peeling off flesh, stinking of death.

The cigar fell from his mouth, struck the box, rolled inside and hit the plastic bag, already full of holes from rough treatment. The cigar burned through the plastic with a hiss. The stink of it filled Hanson's nostrils, and then there was another smell, the smell of burning flesh. He jerked the cigar from the box and stood up quickly.

"Marve, what is it?"

"Baby," his voice was brittle. "Leave the room, please."

"Marve—"

"Trust me. If you've ever trusted me, trust me now."

Rachel stood up from the sofa. "Okay, baby." She exited quickly.

Holding back the bile that was rising in his throat, Hanson opened the box again. He reached in and fished out the folded paper, put it in his lap. He allowed himself three deep breaths of air to clear the smell from his head. He pushed the box away from him with his foot, crushed his cigar out in the ashtray next to the chair.

Unfolded, the note read in cut out letters:

> Your wife or daughter next time, nigger. I'm watching. I'll always be watching. Back off and stay out of my way. The hand belongs to a lovely lady. I have her head and the other hand. I don't even think she's missing yet. Lived alone, from the looks of things. I took my time with her. She may well be my masterpiece. Maybe you can give her relatives a hand. From what I found in the house I believe her name is Patricia. But I won't say anymore. I like to think of her body lying in her house with nothing but the heat. I cut off the air conditioner. It pleases me to think of how it will smell. I may even go back to check on the stench, since I have the key. Hurry up and find her, if you can. Maybe I'll meet you there.
>
> And watch your family, nigger. I like black meat. It goes so well with southern recipes, like Plantation Chicken.
>
> THE HACKER

"God," Hanson said between his teeth. "Oh my God."

Rachel was standing in the doorway of the den. Her lips were trembling ever so slightly. "What is it? Tell me? What's wrong? I know something's wrong."

"JoAnna, where is she?"

Rachel's lips were trembling violently now. "Why?"

"For God's sake, Rachel, tell me."

"The movie."

"Which movie?" Hanson's voice had an edge of impatience to it now.

Rachel shook her head. "I don't know. I told them not to go to the drive-in. An indoor movie somewhere. Please, Marve, what's wrong?"

"JoAnna may be in danger."

"How?"

"I haven't time to explain, just listen to me. I'm going to drive over to that theater on Southmore. It's close, it might be the one. You call the other indoor theaters and have them paged. If you don't locate them, call the drive-in. They may have gone anyway. I know kids."

Rachel quit trembling, seemed to grab hold of her emotions. "Okay."

"I'll explain when I get back, just trust me." Hanson looked at his watch: 10:22. He just might make it to the theater. The features nearly always let out somewhere between 10:30 and 10:45. He hoped for the latter tonight. "I'm going now. You lock the door and do like I said. You don't find them, call the police department, get out an alert for them. Tell them who you are, that your husband's a police officer. Hear?"

Rachel nodded.

"And Rachel?"

"Yes, Marve?"

"Stay away from that box, please?"

Rachel nodded again, as if words were too hard to form.

"I'll explain when I get back. Now start calling."

Almost at a run, Hanson started for the door.

He had killed time accurately. They were coming out of the theater in droves now. The couple he was looking for separated from the crowd and walked arm in arm for the Grand Prix. They were laughing, leaning together. Good. Real good. He was glad they were happy, that would make it all the better when he soured it for them.

Now, if this kid just wasn't a "good" boy that took his date home promptly after a movie, then all would be well . . . for him, anyway.

Tommy and JoAnna got in the Grand Prix. She sat next to him. The sleek automobile moved out on Southmore, pierced the crisp night air like a sharp shadow, the motor humming a soft, contented insect drone.

The blue van followed at a comfortable distance.

"You know," Tommy Rae said, "the part I liked best was where the chick offered Dracula the joint and said this is some good shit . . ."

"And Dracula," JoAnna interjected, "said, I don't smoke shit."

Tommy Rae laughed. "Your Transylvanian accent leaves a little to be desired, but not bad."

Tommy Rae turned off Southmore, headed down a long,

residential street.

The blue van didn't turn off after them. It continued down Southmore at an accelerated speed, shaded a red light, and ran another to the tune of blaring horns and loud curses.

After awhile, the van turned left.

JoAnna, almost in Tommy's lap, began to work her tongue in his ear.

"Hey," Tommy said, "that's not doing much for my driving."

"Then why don't you find a place to park?" JoAnna said.

"Well, I sure ain't takin' you out for a soda."

JoAnna, kissing him on the ear, said, "This isn't the way we usually go."

"Nope. Got a new place. Hell, old Humper's Hill is getting too crowded. They're gonna have to start charging admission. 'Sides, Clarence said he and Lacy got chased out of there by the cops last time they was up there."

"Oh."

"Uh huh, but I've got a humdinger spot. It's . . . "

The screeching of tires distracted him. A blue van wheeled out of a shadowed side street, its lights slicing the Grand Prix like a razor. Then it was behind them, riding close.

"Crazy fool!" Tommy said.

The van bumped the Grand Prix's bumper. Hard!

"Goddamnit!" Tommy said. He stepped on the gas. The Grand Prix leaped forward like a striking cobra. It quickly outdistanced the van by two car lengths, but the van was moving up fast again.

"Can you outrun him?" JoAnna said.

"I don't know. He's got something special under that hood," Tommy said.

"What's he doing?"

"How the fuck do I know? I just met the sonofabitch."

Tommy was moving too fast to take a side street, and the way the van was riding his tail he didn't dare slow down. An island of concrete topped by dirt and grass separated the street. He passed a couple of crossovers but was afraid to take them at such high speed. Except for the Prix and the van, the street was empty of traffic.

The van slammed into their rear again, tossed JoAnna forward into the dash.

"God! You okay?" Tommy said.

JoAnna leaned back holding her head. "Just a bump."

"Get your seat belt on, but first pull mine around me and buckle it."

JoAnna reached across him, fished for the belt, found it, clasped it together around his lean waist.

The van bumped them again.

JoAnna hung to Tommy, then quickly moved to the other side and clamped the passenger's belt around her waist.

The island was ending.

A car was coming down the street now, opposite lane toward them.

"Hang on," Tommy said.

"Jesus," JoAnna said, "you're not going to . . ."

When the car, a white Volkswagen, was almost on them, Tommy jerked a hard left in front of it. Rubber burned and tires screeched. The Grand Prix seemed to lean to the left, almost as if it were trying to do a wheel stand, then suddenly it was level again and moving down a narrow street like a bullet.

The Volkswagen swerved, ran up over the curb and came to rest in a front lawn, its tires buried halfway in grass and dirt.

The van slammed to a stop. Backed fifty feet, stopped again, then quickly turned left after the disappearing taillights of the Grand Prix.

"You could have killed us," JoAnna said.

"No shit. I'm about six inches higher in this seat right now." Tommy checked the rearview mirror. Distant dots of lights were becoming less distant by the second. "The motherfucker's still with us."

The pursuing lights became lamps, then great shimmering moons.

"Christ, I can't outrun the sonofabitch. I'm taking this sucker back out into somewhere."

"There's a precinct station near here," JoAnna said. "Go there. It's not far off. It's on— "

"I know where it is. Hang on, baby, whoever this is, whatever he wants, the bastard's going to have to earn it."

The speedometer was at eighty. The van clamped to their tail as if it were being pulled by the big, sleek car.

"Ever seen someone take a right turn at eighty?"

"Tommy, no, that's crazy."

The Grand Prix seemed to reach around the turn. Tires screamed. Sparks flew out from beneath the car as the axle bounced down and scraped pavement. The car began to skid. The tail end mounted a curb, went up and over, dug down in the soft dirt of a front lawn and hung.

The van didn't attempt to make the crazy turn. It passed by the street, started slowing down for a stop. It took some distance before the van was slow enough to stop, pull in a driveway, and turn around.

Tommy floorboarded the car. It yawned and heaved but remained hung.

The van was picking up speed, making its way toward them.

The front door to the house opened.

JoAnna, looking over her shoulder, saw porchlights come on. "Tommy, someone's up."

Tommy popped his seatbelt off, jerked the door open, stepped out. "Call the police."

It was a man standing in the doorway wearing candy cane pajamas. He had a shotgun in his hand.

"You crazy kids, I'm gonna call the cops."

Tommy was literally hopping up and down. "Great, great, call them."

The van turned at the corner.

214

"Call them," Tommy yelled again and he was back inside the Grand Prix in one smooth motion.

"Tommy," JoAnna whined, "it's the van."

Tommy fastened his seatbelt, slipped the Grand Prix in reverse, gassed it. The Grand Prix rocked. Thick, grey smoke plumed up from the tires and mixed with the night.

The van door opened.

The man in pajamas was yelling something.

All Tommy and JoAnna could hear was the whine of the engine and the digging of the tires.

JoAnna looked at the van. A dark shape, a man, was stepping from it. She couldn't make out his features. He was wearing some kind of long coat, and now as he came from the van, he flipped a hood up and over his head. Was he wearing a raincoat?

The car backed out of the ruts slowly, digging a longer trench as it went.

The man in the pajamas discharged his shotgun in the air.

The man from the van jerked his head at the house, saw the man standing there. He had been so wrapped up in his quarry, he had noticed neither lights nor the man.

Tommy jerked the Grand Prix in drive and eased down on the gas, then floorboarded it again. The car jumped out of the self-made ruts, bounced over the curb and was off.

The man in the raincoat leaped back in the van. JoAnna, looking out the back window, thought she saw something in his hand. Something long and shiny.

In less than thirty seconds the van was hot on their tires again.

Tommy tried to keep his speed moderate. The van bumped them twice, once nearly forcing them off the road. It was pulling around them on the left.

"Let him pass, Tommy, let him pass."

"Pass, hell! He wants our ass. Another coat of paint and we'll be wearing that van."

The van was pulling up neck and neck now. The driver of the van, the hood pulled up over his head, looked like some kind of monk.

"Why, why, why?" JoAnna said.

"Who am I, Hurkos?" Tommy growled. "Sorry, babe."

The street was opening out into the highway now. Lights were abundant.

"Tommy, this hill is too damn steep."

"Shut up and pray nothing is coming."

The road suddenly started down. Tommy made no effort to check his speed. He held the pedal to the floor. The great black car leaped out into space and dove down the other side, seemed to fall a great distance before the tires touched pavement again. The force of impact nearly jerked Tommy out of his seatbelt, but he stayed with the wheel, trying to remember and respond to the old adage of turning in the direction of the skid.

Out into the busy highway the car went, whipping its tail to the left, very fast. It looked like an elongated, black top with yellow eyes whirling aroundandaroundandaround.

A tire blew. The naked wheel, flapping slabs of black rubber around it like hooked fish, tore up concrete and popped up sparks to the height of ten feet.

Half a dozen cars barely avoided hitting the Grand Prix before it rolled twice, then came to rest on the opposite side of the highway lying on its right side.

The van, which had checked its speed before the hill, cruised down slowly, turned right and headed off unnoticed.

4

SATURDAY . . . 11:15 p.m.

Frustrated, disappointed, he ditched the van near his car, shed his raincoat and concealed the bayonet within its folds. His hands were shaking. He had been cheated of his prize. He had given them fear, but he had not satiated his urge. That came only with the work of his blade, with the spilling of dark red blood.

He walked the short distance to his car, his footsteps thudding in his ears like frightened heartbeats.

Over and over Rachel told herself to be calm.

Her fingers weren't listening. They kept twitching and crawling together with their companions, wringing, clenching. She sat next to the phone, leaning in her chair as though ready to leap.

She had called all the theaters, even the Houston ones. Paging had accomplished nothing. She had even tried the drive-ins. Same lack of results. Next she had called the police station and explained that her husband was a police officer and that they were trying to find their daughter. And then she had done what Marvin had asked her not to do.

She had looked in the box.

After a trip to the bathroom to discharge the contents of her stomach, she had returned to the box, and this time with her emotions in control, she read the note.

The Hacker. The Houston Fiend was after her baby.

God, Marve . . . call, come home with the kids, something. Anything.

She thought of Joe Clark. He was a cop, Marve's best friend. Maybe he could do something. What, she didn't know, but she was ready to clutch at straws.

Quickly now, dial and state the problem, then get off, don't tie up the line. She suddenly realized that she was calling Joe for comfort. She needed to reach out and know someone was on the other end.

She dialed his number.

The phone rang several times.

No one answered.

At 11:44 Hanson came in the door. Rachel almost ran to meet him. There was no one with him. She asked the question. Hanson looked at her for a long, silent moment, then said:

"Nothing. Not a goddamned thing!"

"Oh Christ!" Rachel said, and she began to cry.

His eyes wet with tears, Hanson went to her and held her.

"You did what I asked?" he said.

"Yes," Rachel said tearfully. "Nothing. The police are search-ing."

"Good." He patted her back and pulled her hair close to his face, smelled her gentle frangrance. "They'll find them."

She lifted her head and looked him squarely in the eyes. "Alive? I read the note."

Hanson couldn't say anything.

"The Hacker, Marve. The Hacker is after us because of you."

Swallowing, he said, "I know. I'm going to call the Pasadena station, tell them about the note."

Rachel allowed Hanson to move away from her, and when he was nearly to the den she said, "I have already. When I read the note I called them back."

"You saw . . . what was in the box?"

She nodded.

"I'm sorry," Hanson said.

"If anything happens to JoAnna, don't use that word. Don't use any words. They won't help." Rachel turned and walked to the kitchen.

Hanson watched her go. He suddenly realized that in his haste to find JoAnna he had left Rachel alone. She would have been at the mercy of the madman. He was losing his head. Time after time.

"God," he said aloud, and he began to tremble.

✦   ✦   ✦

There were so many lights it looked like Christmas. Red, blue, yellow and white splashed abstract designs against the canvas of night.

The street was filled with automobiles: halted traffic — many of the occupants outside their machines staring gooseneck over the tops of cars and the heads of people — police cars, ambulances, a wrecker, and two lime green fire trucks. Shortly thereafter came Barlowe of *The Bugle*.

Barlowe abandoned his car, and using shoulders and press card, made his way through the throng of on-lookers and up to the boundary that authorities had made with their vehicles and personnel.

The Grand Prix was lying on its side. It looked like some kind of giant bug about to flip over on its back, but trying desperately not to. A firetruck had pulled up on the roof side and pushed its butt against it to keep it from rocking on over and smashing down on its top. A wrecker supported the other side. Two firemen swarmed up the wrecker wench and came down on the car's side, peered through the glass. Inside they could see two unconscious forms, the closest, a teenage boy, dangled downwards, held in place by his seatbelt. The other, a girl, lay with her head against the smashed passenger window. There was blood mixed with the shattered glass.

One of the firemen tried the door. No go. When the car had rolled the door had been crushed. It would have to be cut open, or with a little luck they could lower the Grand Prix down and go in from the girl's side.

They set about attaching the wrecker's grappling device to the underside of the car, next to the driver's door. When the hook was fastened securely, the firefighters climbed down.

Barlowe yelled to one of the bunkersuited firemen who had climbed down from the Grand Prix.

"Bad?"

The fireman looked at him. Barlowe waved his press card, inched around two policemen without resistance. The police were accustomed to the press, and especially Barlowe. He was a familiar figure to them.

Barlowe made his way over to the man, repeated, "Bad?"

"Could be," the man answered. "Couple of kids in there. Neither are moving. Man, you press guys get here quick."

Barlowe smiled. "Police radio in my car helps. I was out this way already."

The firefighter nodded. "Well, excuse me, I think they're just about ready for me." With that he strode away from Barlowe toward the Grand Prix and the wrecker.

The wrecker driver, watching and working carefully, was pulling away from the Grand Prix, tugging it forward, keeping the winch taut. When the once sleek automobile was hanging by support of the wrecker alone, its right side tires just touching the pavement, the winch began to slowly unwind. Carefully, the driver settled the car into an upright position.

That done, the two firemen that had climbed on the car and

looked inside, ran out to try the passenger door.

No dice. The roll had frozen it as well.

The burly firefighter who had spoken to Barlowe turned and yelled something to a crowd of men. A moment later one ran forward holding an instrument that at first glance looked like some kind of chainsaw. Barlowe recognized it immediately. It was a gas driven tool, nicknamed The Jaws of Life, and in less than three minutes it could pull the door off the Grand Prix as easily as a knife sliding through peanut butter.

As the fireman began working on the boy's side the air was suddenly full of the machine's engine whine; and shortly thereafter, the screech of its "jaws" chewing metal.

Less than three mintues later the fireman moved back and killed the machine. The door was off.

A paramedic ran forward and leaned into the car, checked the boy's pulse. He took a stethoscope from around his neck, slipped the ends in his ears, put it to the boy's throat, then moved it to his chest. After a moment he straightened himself up and moved from the car.

"Unfasten the seatbelt and take him out," the paramedic said. "This kid's dead."

Two large firemen responded, and then, as the boy was removed and laid out beside the car, the paramedic crawled across the seat to the girl.

One of the firemen said, "Boy's neck is broken, I think."

"Looks that way," the other one said.

From inside the car the paramedic yelled, "This one's alive."

SUNDAY ... 12:05 a.m.

The phone rang. Hanson picked it up promptly. His voice was a dry croak. "Hello."

"Is this the Hanson residence?"

"It is."

Rachel, who had been sitting in the kitchen draped over a cup of cold coffee, came into the room the moment the phone rang.

"Lieutenant, this is Sergeant Fierd at the Pasadena Police Department."

"Yes," Hanson said weakly.

"There's been an accident, I'm afraid."

"God. JoAnna?"

"Yes, but she's fine. Nothing more than a good bump. I'm afraid the boy is dead. Car turned over."

"But JoAnna is all right?"

Rachel was saying over and over, "What is it, Marve? What is it?"

"She's all right," Fierd said. "She's in Bayshore."

"Thank you, Sergeant. We're on our way now."

5

SUNDAY . . . 1:30 a.m.

The hospital clock said 1:30. Hanson paced the sterile aisles like a test rat in search of the cheese. Rachel sat quietly in one of the hall chairs clenching her hands. She was clenching so tightly the circulation in them was nearly dead.

Rachel watched Hanson. He had aged ten years overnight it seemed, and her earlier comment certainly hadn't helped him any. She licked her dry lips, said, "Marve."

He stopped pacing. "Yes?"

"What I said earlier. I'm sorry. I was upset. I didn't mean it."

He smiled. "That's all right. It was well deserved. I have been acting foolish."

"I said he was after us because of you. You're just doing your job. I'm sorry."

"Forget it."

"Marve?"

"Yes?"

"I truly am sorry."

Hanson went over and sat in the chair beside her, held her cold hands in one of his. "It's going to be all right. You'll see."

"You think it was The Hacker that caused the wreck?"

Hanson shook his head. "I don't know. Just know what Fierd told me and what the doctor said."

"She did say a man was chasing them. A man in a blue van with a raincoat."

"That's what the doctor said. But she was hysterical when she came to. A bump on the head . . . "

"You don't believe that. It was The Hacker."

"Yeah," Hanson said. "I believe it was."

They both turned to the sudden squeaking of soft shoes. Their family doctor, a short, plump man in his fifties, was coming down the corridor. His face always looked flushed and his nose was the brightest part of it.

Hanson stood up, said almost before the doctor was in hearing distance. "How is she?"

"Mr. and Mrs. Hanson," he said as way of greeting, ignoring Hanson's question.

"Doctor Bran," Hanson said, "how is she?"

"Fine, fine, fine. Healthy girl. Strong. She's in a bit of shock, of course."

"Does she know about, Tommy?" Rachel said.

"No, no. Of course not. Wouldn't want to mention that just now. Told her the boy was in intensive care. She's asked about him several times."

"Shouldn't we just tell her?" Hanson said.

"No. Don't think so. Bad time for that. Shock, you know. Crazy stuff," Bran said, pulling his earlobe.

"JoAnna will be all right?" Rachel asked.

"Fit as a fiddle. Fine. Fine." The doctor paused, looked about as if watching for spies. "Tell you what, and let's not make a big announcement out of this, but I want you to take that gal home."

"Home?" Hanson said. "But you said she was in shock . . . "

"Oh shut up," Bran said pleasantly. "I'm the goddamned doctor around here. Want to see my license?"

Hanson smiled. "No. I seem to remember you delivering JoAnna."

"And they say elephants have a memory? Now you folks listen to me and stay shushed up 'til I get finished. I'm anxious to get my old tired butt home. I'd like to eat, too. I'm so damn hungry I can see corn bread walkin' on the ground. Now, JoAnna is in a state of shock. Common, of course, very common in an incident like this. Hospital would love for you to keep her here for observation, lots more money in that. I want to save you folks some money and I want to do JoAnna some good.

"Tonight that nut in the van, whoever he was, put the fear of the Lord into her. She needs to be home. She'll feel more comfortable there. She ain't sleeping worth an owl hoot right now anyway. Too nervous, shock, different surroundings. Do her a whale of good to spend the night in her own bed. That all right with you folks?"

"Fine with me," Rachel said quickly.

"You sure it's all right? I mean, it won't do her any harm?"

"Think I'd make much of a living killing off my patients, son?"

"No sir."

"Then shut up and let's check that kid of yours out. Someone in a bad way might need that bed."

"Lieutenant," a voice called from the end of the hall. The trio turned. A handsome man in his fifties had just stepped out of the elevator, walking briskly their way. He wore a three hundred dollar suit, dark brown with a matching tie against a dark green shirt. His highly polished brown shoes caught the light and threw it away as he walked. It was Captain Fredricks.

"Captain," Hanson said.

Fredricks held out his hand, shook with Hanson, Bran and finally Rachel. To her he said, "Been awhile since I've seen you."

"Yes, it has."

Fredricks took on a sour expression. "Sorry about the circumstances."

"She's quite all right," Rachel said.

"That's good," Fredricks answered, "that's very good." After a moment of awkward silence Fredricks said, "If I can be forgiven for this, is it possible that the Lieutenant and I could be alone for a moment, to talk something over. I'm afraid it's private."

"Why don't you," Doctor Bran said. "Me and your missus will get the check-out business over with. All kinds of doodly-do before you can get someone out of one of these institutions." Bran took Rachel's arm. "Come on, Mrs. Hanson, and try to look like my date. I'd like to give them snooty young doctors something to think about."

Rachel laughed. "Silly."

"Go ahead," Hanson said. "I'll be along."

"Nobody is worrying about you," Doctor Bran said, and he and Rachel, arm in arm, went down the corridor.

"I'm afraid this is a bit of a business matter, personal too. I got a call on this from Fierd over at the Pasadena station . . . "

"I'm sorry he called. There was no need for him to bother you at this time of night."

"Don't even say it. I like to keep tabs on my folks. Makes for a better team. First off, I'm really sorry about what happened."

"Thank you. I got a note, and a box . . . I turned them over to the Pasadena police. They were supposed to take my key and go by . . . "

"They did. I've talked to Fierd about it. Terrible thing to get in the mail. We're looking for the girl's body now. No idea where to look, of course, but we've got missing person reports out. That might draw in something."

"But this isn't what you came here to talk to me about, is it?"

"Not exactly." Fredricks waved his hand at the lobby chairs. "Let's sit a minute."

When they were seated Fredricks said, "Your daughter supposedly mumbled something to the paramedic about a man trying to kill them, trying to force them off the road."

"Correct."

"Well, we're certain that man was The Hacker."

"Certain?"

"Pasadena station got a phone call. It was from The Hacker. He admitted to it, said, 'I'm going to get the nigger and his family tonight.'"

"Jesus H. Christ!"

"It may just be talk, but it's a threat. I'd like to ask you a favor. You can decline if you like, and you may want to after I explain."

"Ask away," Hanson said.

"I want you to play like the bait in the trap."

"I don't follow altogether."

"You and Rachel go home and act like you know nothing about the phone call, or at least not that you're concerned. We're going to post men outside and inside the house. You'll have plenty of protection."

"If he's a cop he'll know that. He might even be one of the men."

"No. I've thought of that. It's occured to me that he might know of our plans, but if he's as screwy as he seems, he just might try anyway, and I'll pick cops who have airtight alibis for the days of the murders. If he tries we've got him. If not, well, I sleep better knowing you're safe. Matter of fact, I'm anticipating a bit. I've already had your house thoroughly searched in case he's lying in wait, and I've posted the cops. Got four on the outside — two in front across the street, and two out back. Got two men inside, or will have. Just one right now. I'm going to add a man to that."

"And you'll have me."

Fredricks was silent a moment. "Lieutenant. You're a good cop, but I don't want you on this thing."

"What?"

"You'll be in the house, of course . . . But I don't even want you carrying a gun."

"It's my family."

"That's why I don't want you totin' iron. Lieutenant — and I don't mean this unkindly — you've been a little, how do they say? Off your feed as of late."

Hanson opened his mouth to complain but said nothing. He remembered how he had run off and left Rachel alone. He had been in a blind panic.

"You're right," Hanson said. "You're absolutely right."

6

SUNDAY . . . 2:30 a.m.

Without his gun hugging his ribs, Hanson felt sexually neutered. He hated to admit there was anything to that man and his gun stuff, but it was almost as if someone had ripped away his manhood in one brutal swipe. He had been carrying that Colt Python for so long it seemed like a part of him.

Was he that bad? That tense? Surely they didn't think he was going to snap and start shooting cops and family. No. More likely they feared he'd pot-shoot The Hacker if he showed up. And he would have, too.

He sat quietly in the dark at the dining room table shuffling a deck of cards in a slow, whispery manner. It was just something to do with his hands. It was too dark to see the face of the cards as well. Across from him, hands in lap, making no more movement than a stuffed iguana, was a detective-sergeant named Raul Martinez. He was one of the inside duty men; the other had yet to show up.

Few words had passed between Hanson and Martinez, and much of the reason was that too much talk might discourage The Hacker should he come lurking out of the dark and up to the house for a looksee and a listen.

No matter what the reason, Hanson was grateful for the silence. He wasn't in a mood to talk. He was in a mood to think. It hardly seemed likely to him that The Hacker would try anything. The guy was no fool. He wouldn't call and not expect the police to act just as they were acting; especially if he himself were a cop. But then madmen were not to be figured.

What was it old Doc Warren had said, something about this man being intelligent, a cold and calculating killer? Something like that. And that being the case, he wasn't going to walk willy-nilly into any simple trap.

Then why the threat? Was it to keep Houston's finest on their collective toes? It didn't make sense. Unless it was a cop who delighted in plaguing the department.

That made him wonder. The thought had been there before, almost surfaced like a bloated drowning victim several times, but he had held it under. He let it surface now. The thought became totally alive. The thought was: was The Hacker Joe?

It seemed so unlikely. He knew Joe well. Joe was his closest friend. But things added up. Like tonight, Rachel told him she had called Joe for comfort, but that there was no answer. Him not being home, or not answering, didn't make him The Hacker, but it certainly added to suspicion.

Hanson began to sort the characteristics Warren had given him, put them in order with what he knew about Joe.

Warren said that The Hacker was most likely a loner. Joe was certainly that. Hanson didn't even know where he lived and he was his best friend. Joe had suffered a major trauma in his life when his marriage had fallen through. He was constantly trying to discourage violent thought and action on Hanson's part. Maybe it was just because Hanson was overly obsessed with the killer, or maybe it was because Joe was trying to make things easier on himself. Could it have been him that talked to the captain about his outburst in Evans' office, instead of Barlowe or Evans himself? Made sense. It certainly could be Joe.

Christ! Joe? The man who was his partner? The man he called friend?

Stop that kind of thinking, he told himself. It's ridiculous.

But the thought wouldn't go away. The idea grew like mold the more Hanson considered it.

SUNDAY . . . 2:45 a.m.

They were fools, absolute fools to think they could outsmart him. And they would try. Did they think him so stupid as not to expect police protection for Hanson's family?

No. He wasn't a fool. He wanted it that way. It added to the game, the fun.

No. He wasn't a fool. He was hungry. That's what he was. Hungry to give pain and to see and taste blood.

SUNDAY . . . 2:46 a.m.

Joe Clark's phone rang. He answered it on the first ring.

"Hello," Clark said.

"This is Captain Fredricks."

"Yes, Captain."

"Excuse the hour."

"No problem. I don't sleep worth a good goddamn anyway. Insomnia."

"This is important or I wouldn't have called."

"Hit me with it."

Briefly, but with great accuracy, Fredricks told Clark the events of the night, the threat and the precautions he had taken.

"And JoAnna is okay?" Clark asked.

"As well as can be expected. The doctor thought she'd do better at home."

"Good."

"What?"

"Good. Good she's home. I suppose you have something you want me to do?"

"Yeah. One reason I want you for what I have in mind is that you and Hanson are close. Actually, I think there are enough men there already, five to be exact, two out front, two at the back and one inside. But I promised Hanson two inside. I want that other man to be you, someone he knows, feels comfortable with, and can trust. I meant to get you there earlier, but couldn't get hold of you."

"I went to a movie."

"Yeah, well, I want you inside. I don't have to tell you that I think Hanson is close to cracking down. I took him off the case and even had him hand over his gun."

"That right?"

"Yeah. He's ripe for stupidity these days."

239

"Yes, sir. Afraid that's true."

"That day you told me about the outburst in Evans' office, I should have taken his ass off the case then. Immediately. I don't think I've done him a bit of good, or the investigation, by keeping him on."

"You used your best judgement, sir. Gorilla — Lieutenant Hanson — has always been a fine officer; lately he's just had some pressure. I don't know why. In the field too long, maybe."

"Thanks, Sergeant. Now get over there and park out of sight, walk up to the house. I'll call Mitchel and tell him you're coming. He's in an old Volkswagen bus parked across the street against the curb. You'll find him and Tyler easy enough."

"On my way. And sir?"

"Yes."

"Thanks."

"All right. I knew you'd want to be close to the lieutenant at a time like this."

"You got that right on the head, sir."

"Best of luck."

"Yeah. So long, Captain."

They both hung up.

7

SUNDAY . . . 2:51 a.m.

When there is emotional pain mixed with anticipation the hours crawl by like crippled snails. The minutes seem to hang forever, and thoughts, worn and frazzled at the edges, haunt the corridors of the brain like a restless and malignant spirit.

Thoughts of Joe. Thoughts of The Hacker. They danced through Hanson's mind like waltzing mice, blended together and became one. It had to be, he concluded. It had to be.

The phone rang him out of his mental well.

As was planned they let the phone ring five times. This was to convince The Hacker, should he call to taunt or threaten, that the family was asleep. On the other hand, if the phone were answered promptly, the killer might smell a trap.

Upstairs, the phone rang in the master bedroom in unison

with the phone below. Rachel sat upright in bed, listened. The ringing of the phone was like knife jabs in the heart. Could it be . . . *him?* Fredricks had said The Hacker might call; that he enjoyed those little games, pleasured in the anxiety they caused.

Beside her JoAnna slept a drugged sleep. Sound as a rock. The phone was not in her world.

Rachel became so wrapped up in her fearful thoughts she almost didn't notice when the phone quit ringing.

"Hanson residence," Hanson said.

"Barlowe, Lieutenant."

The phone was less than six feet away from Martinez, and Martinez was leaning forward, listening intently.

"What the hell you calling at this hour for?"

"Phone tapped?"

"No."

"Something you ought to know. Can you act casual?"

"I think so."

"Do it. This is an emergency, but I think it's something you'll want to know alone."

"Just a minute." Hanson turned to Martinez. "No sweat. Guy callin' for me to go over and play cards."

Martinez nodded, leaned back in his chair and resumed his stuffed iguana impersonation.

"Don't think I'm up to playing cards, Harry. I mean, hell, man. You woke me up."

"I need to see you."

"Not tonight."

"This is as important as hell. Say what you got to to make it look good, but listen to this and memorize. Get to this address, quickly." Barlowe read it off.

Between pauses Hanson said, "Uh huh, uh huh. Another time, Harry." Then very carefully. "Why cards tonight?"

"I know who the goddamned Hacker is. That's why tonight!" Barlowe hung up.

Hanson went on talking like nothing had happened. "Quite all right. I'm just a bit cranky when I get woke up. I know I was supposed to be there. Yeah. Yeah. Uh huh. Bye."

"Who was that?" Martinez asked.

"Friend. I usually play cards this night of the week."

Martinez frowned. "This time of the morning?"

"Harry doesn't pay attention to his watch. He just likes cards. He's got the gang over there and he's short on dough. He wanted me to come over and lend him some. He didn't really give a hoot in hell if I wanted to play cards or not. When it comes to money, he doesn't give a damn about a man's rest."

Martinez smiled an expansive smile. "I got a cousin like that."

"Yeah, well you know the score then."

It suddenly occurred to Hanson what he was going to do. He couldn't tell Martinez the truth, lest the sergeant suspect his motives. Of course he could tell the truth, have a cop sent to the address, find out from Barlowe what the scoop was. But no way. If Barlowe knew who The Hacker was, Hanson wanted to be sure

243

he was the next to know. He wished more than ever that he had a gun.

"You know," Martinez said suddenly, "Captain should have tapped the phone."

"I guess. He wasn't sure he could trust everybody in that department. Wanted only those he could be certain weren't The Hacker."

"Well, we fill the bill. All got air-tight alibis. 'Sides, it ain't no cop."

"You sound awful certain," Hanson said.

"Just don't think it's a cop."

"Guy sure seems to know a lot about our operations, seems to always be a step ahead of us." Hanson realized he was pacing. He went back to his chair, tried to look calm, but not too calm.

"Nothing he couldn't do by just usin' common sense," Martinez said. "That's always the first thing people think of in a nut case. It's a cop. Remember Son of Sam? That's what they said about him."

"Who the hell knows," Hanson said flatly. Then after a moment, Hanson looked at his watch, made a big production of looking bored. "I'm going down to the 7-11. It's open all night. I want to get some cigars . . . and maybe a beer. Since I'm not officially on the case I think I could do with one. Especially after tonight. Want anything?"

Martinez licked his lips. "How about bringing me a beer that you won't even notice me drinking?"

"Won't even see you. What kind you want?"

"Schlitz."

"Cow piss."

"Not to me," Martinez said.

"I might take awhile," Hanson warned. "Once in a rare moon that place closes at eleven, just like its name implies. If so, I'll go on up Southmore. I know another place. I may be awhile, now. I like to look through the magazine rack pretty thoroughly."

"Take you time, man."

"This isn't going to get you in any trouble?"

"Naw. I wasn't told to make you no prisoner, just to watch for The Hacker. He'd be a fool to show up."

Hanson knew that wasn't entirely the truth. Martinez wanted that beer. He wanted to get out of there before Martinez suggested getting it himself.

"True enough," Hanson said. "He would be a fool to show up." Hanson stood up. "I'll be back in a little while."

"No sweat."

"Lock the door behind me."

"Sure."

Hanson went to the door and out. Martinez called to him, "I'll radio out to Mitchel. He gets kind of thirsty, too."

Hanson smiled. "I'll make it a six-pack, better yet, two six-packs." Hanson started walking toward the car.

Martinez locked the door, went back to the table and picked up the walkie-talkie, radioed Mitchel. Mitchel liked the idea. He was thirsty, and he was sure the others would be as well.

Martinez, putting the walkie-talkie aside, thought Hacker

Smacker. No way that bastard is going to show up here.

There just wasn't any way he could have known.

8

SUNDAY . . . 3:25 a.m. AND COUNTING

The night was as soft as a woman's breast. The air was full of the smell of rain; a smell that reminded Hanson of the country, of his granddaddy's farm. But tonight it seemed more like the odor of a fresh dug grave, the clinging stench of a funeral shroud.

Hanson stood on his front lawn taking in the night; watching dark clouds boil in over the moon. After a moment he went out to his car, waved to the Volkswagen bus across the street. He couldn't see the cop, Mitchel, inside, but he knew he was there; knew walkie-talkies were crackling, communicating with Martinez inside.

He knew Martinez would radio the others about the beer. He had been on many stakeouts himself. He, however, never drank when working, not even a beer. Nor would he tolerate anyone working under him drinking on the job.

Right now he was grateful for human weakness and the fruit of the grain. By the time they realized he had been gone too long for beer, cigars, or even magazine looking, it would be too late.

It only took a moment to kill.

Joe Clark, raincoat tucked firmly beneath his arm, came out of his apartment and walked briskly to his parked car. He stopped, examined the clouds overhead, sniffed the air. There was the stench of the city mixed with the smell of on-coming rain. Above, the heavens slashed open briefly to reveal a thin, short-lived fork of yellow-white lightning.

Yep, he'd need the raincoat. He tossed it in the front seat, climbed in.

A moment later he was heading for the Hanson residence, the rain falling against his windshield in small, wet pearls.

Barlowe waited in the room with one of the corpses for awhile, then went out and stood among the shadowed shrubbery. He checked his watch; thought it won't be long now.

Rachel couldn't sleep, couldn't even rest. It was as if she sensed the collapsing of the universe. Certainly, her own personal universe had folded.

She checked JoAnna. Still lost in the ozone.

Rachel climbed out of bed, slipped her feet in house shoes. She went to the bedroom window and looked out. It was raining. Not hard, just steadily. The streetlights made the side lawn and the neighbor's roof glisten. It was almost as if the yard had been sprinkled with glitter.

Rachel let the curtain slide back into position. Would morning ever come?

At precisely the same time, Captain Fredricks radioed Sergeant Mitchel in the Volkswagen bus, informed him that Joe Clark was on his way and that he was to be the second inside man. He then asked how Hanson and the family were.

"Asleep. All asleep," Mitchell lied.

"Good, and I'm fixin' to be, too, just as soon as I can get back to the house."

Fredricks signed off, turned off his car radio and went back inside. He could sleep soundly now. All was well.

Mitchel used his walkie-talkie to contact Martinez.

"Where the fuck's Hanson?"

"I told you. He went out for beer."

"He's taking his sweetass time. The Captain just called. I lied. Told him Hanson was asleep. He finds out and it's my ass and I'm takin' yours with me."

"It's all our asses. But don't sweat. He'll be back. He said he was going to take his time."

"You should never have let him out of the house."

"No sweat," Martinez said, but his voice lacked conviction. "It'll all come out in the wash."

"Try this on for size. Fredricks is sending over Joe Clark to be the second man inside."

"Yeah. Now?"

"Now. I don't know him, but they say he's one good cop, sticks pretty tight by the rules."

"I've seen him. But if he's Hanson's partner he won't rat. Like father like son, like partner like partner."

"Yeah, well remember, your partner's off the force. Little something about accepting a bribe."

"Go to hell, Mitchell."

"We'll be better in hell than anywhere else if Fredricks gets wind of this," Mitchel clicked off.

Shit, Martinez thought to himself. Mitchel's in a panic. Everything's cool. Hanson will be back shortly, and Clark's bound to be one of the boys. He'll want a beer like the rest of us.

Sure, one of the boys.

9

SUNDAY . . . 4 a.m. AND COUNTING

An ornamental brick wall showed briefly in the headlights. It broke open into a drive. Hanson whipped in and killed the lights almost in the same move.

No other car was visible. The garage was locked up tight. There were no lights in the house and no one was waiting in the drive. Only the shrubbery seemed alive, swaying and whipping to the beat of the rain and the gust of the wind.

Hanson sat a moment, considered. Perhaps he had the address wrong. He was thinking it over when a shadow disengaged itself from the shrubbery and the door on the passenger's side jerked open.

✦   ✦   ✦

It wasn't cold in the house, but Rachel shivered.

She hadn't even tried to go back to bed. Instead, driven by a strange, uncontrollable fear, she had gone to the closet and found a large, brown, paper bag. She set it on her dresser and reached inside, took a hammer from amongst hundreds of loose nails. She had used the hammer and nails to install her new curtains three months ago. She had not even thought of the hammer until now; until fear and gloom settled on her like the dark shadow of death.

She felt the weight of the hammer in her palm.

God, she was considering hitting someone with it. Could she do it?

She looked at JoAnna sleeping.

Uh huh. She could do it.

Joe Clark checked his watch: 4:15. Not much farther. Another fifteen or twenty minutes to Pasadena, and then maybe twenty minutes more. He shook out a cigarette and lit it with the car lighter. He smoked calmly. Drove reasonably.

Hanson was startled at first, but then he realized the wet figure sliding in beside him was Barlowe.

"What the . . . " Hanson began.

"Make the block," Barlowe said quickly.

"Look . . . "

"Just make the fuckin' block, all right?"

Hanson stared at Barlowe a moment. "All right," he said. He backed out and started around the block, driving slowly.

"You know this place?" Barlowe asked.

"The address?"

"Yeah, yeah. Do you know it?"

"No. First time I've been here."

"I know you know a guy named Milo in Evidence."

"I know him."

"That's his house."

"Okay. That's Milo's house. You tryin' to tell me he's the man I want?"

"No. I'm trying to tell you he's dead, mothafucker."

"What?"

"Just drive and listen . . . Go on down this block, make two or three, this might take a bit."

"You call the cops? . . . What's this got to do with anything?"

"It's got to do with The Hacker, asshole, and you're a cop. I called you, didn't I? First off. I don't like your black ass at all, and I don't give a fuck about you. I want this scoop. That's the deal. Plain and simple. But this can help us both. You want to listen?"

"Tell me all about it."

"All right. Here's the telegram version. Milo was selling evidence to me."

"So it was him?"

"Uh huh. I was using what he gave me to write my articles. A cop, your partner, Joe Clark got wise to what Milo was doing. Milo tried to swear off the dirty bucks, but he couldn't. He had that cretin kid."

"Not a cretin. He has cerebral palsy."

"A damn geek, anyway. He needed the money. He kept coming back for more. He told me this Clark was on his ass closer'n a dingleberry. He was worried sick. Tonight he calls me, says, look I've got something for you. I told him I thought he'd said it was all over. He said it was, but this one was a biggie. Could I get him a thousand? I told him I could get him a thousand about the same time I sprouted a new set of ears. And then he says, for this you can. I know who The Hacker is.

"I tell him, all right, if it's good enough I can get you the jack. But this better not be no con. I don't go much for gettin' up in the middle of the night for no con. He says, this is the straight goods.

"So I drive over here. Lights were on. The door was unlocked. No one answered the bell. I leaned on the door and went in. I found the jello kid in the hallway. His brains are all over the wall. The old gal's in the back bedroom, same condition, and Milo was in his study, what was left of his head is all over the desk. There was an automatic with a silencer in his hand."

"Suicide."

"Nope. A plant. No nitrate smell on the hand, and the gun's been forced into it. The finger on the trigger guard has a bruise on it and the nail's snapped off. Someone killed the kid and the old lady and Milo. Tried to make it look like a suicide. The

Hacker's who."

"That's not his style."

"The bastard's no fool, Hanson. He knew Milo was onto him. He must have planned on getting him tonight. Milo waited until he was sure his family was asleep, then called me. Just so happened he got the call to me before The Hacker arrived to kill the family and rig the suicide."

"Jesus."

"I know for sure it was The Hacker. The evidence is in the house. I could have brought it out, but I wanted you to see it, shall we say, in its natural habitat."

"We need to call the law in."

"We will. When I found the bodies I cut the lights and waited out in the shrubbery for you. My car's parked down the block from Milo's. I think you should park behind it and we should walk up. Safer that way."

"All right, Barlowe. But if you're trying to be cute, I'm going to snap your neck like a dry chicken bone."

"Don't say," Barlowe said. "Excuse me while I perspire with fear."

Hanson clenched his teeth, remained silent. He drove around the block and back toward Milo's place. He stopped when Barlowe said, "That's my car over there. Pull up behind it."

Hanson parked, got out. Barlowe stood with his arms resting on the open door, the rain beating down on him. He pinched a package of cigarettes out of his shirt pocket, shook a damp one out. He fumbled with the pack, dropped it back inside the car.

Hanson came around in front of the car. Watching Barlowe he couldn't resist, "Old Hard as Nails Barlowe isn't nervous is he?"

Barlowe bent down across the seat, came up with his cigarettes.

"No," he said calmly closing the car door. "Just clumsy. 'Sides, sumbitches is soaked." He pushed the damp cigarette back into the pack, slipped it in his pocket.

"Come on," Hanson said. "I'm drowning."

The two men walked briskly toward the house.

Inside was the smell of death, blood and excrement. The movies give death glamour. A body flailing back from the force of a shot, a sudden stream of blood squirting up. In real life it's uglier, far uglier. At the instant of death the sphincter muscles often let go. There's the sudden nauseous smell of internal gases and excrement. The body sometimes twists and knots into convulsive positions, hardens as rigor mortis sets in. Humanity leaves the body like a butterfly leaves a cocoon. What remains is a shell. A hard, dead, stinking shell.

That was what was left of the Milo family. Shells.

The boy was in the hall. Crusting gore and grey matter clung to the wall behind him. He was clothed in pajamas. His head was a mess; like a ripe watermelon dropped from twenty stories.

Hanson turned on his cop stomach. He had seen it many times. He never ever got used to it.

Barlowe seemed as bored as a tour guide. He led Hanson down the hall to a back bedroom. The door was open. Barlowe took out his wallet, used the edge of it to flick on the light.

A woman — her body led Hanson to believe she had been in her thirties — lay on the bed, dressed only in underpants. There was not the least bit of seductiveness about her. She had half a face. The right side of her head was an explosion of blood and gristle. The shot had entered her right eye. Around her head was a mushroom cloud of grey matter and gore matted with flesh and hair.

Barlowe walked over to the body. "I think," he said, "that the shot was delivered while she slept. Close range." Barlowe raised his hand and pointed his finger at the woman. "Bang. Like that."

"We'll get snapshots for your collection later. Come on. Get out of here. Show me what you're going to show me and let's call some law."

"Sure," Barlowe said, shrugging. He followed Hanson out, used his wallet to flick off the light.

"This way," Barlowe said, and he edged around Hanson, walked briskly, his tour guide role resumed.

Milo lay on the floor next to the overturned study chair. Using his handkerchief, Hanson turned on the desk lamp. There was blood all over the desk. He took a good look at Milo. The shot had entered just above his right ear and come out near the top of his head on the left side. It looked as if some huge and ravenous animal had eaten its way out of his skull. The flesh was folded back and a glob of brains swelled out of his head. The eyes were the color of sun-dried slate.

Hanson went around behind the desk and knelt down close to the body, examined the hand that held the automatic with silencer. Barlowe was right. He had to give the ghoulish bastard credit for that. The gun had been forced into Milo's hand.

"Figure the kid heard something," Barlowe said, "waddled out of his room for a look and caught a slug. The killer then killed Milo and after that the wife, came back in here and tried to rig the gun for a suicide.

Hanson nodded. "Looks that way."

"Now here's the interesting part. Milo must have been writing out what he knew on this pad." Barlowe picked a pencil from his soaked shirt pocket and tapped a yellow legal pad on Milo's desk. "The killer, having done what he set out to do, took what Milo was writing. You see, Milo was going to hand over the evidence to me. I'd give him the thousand, and the paper would get a big scoop."

"Get on with it, Barlowe. This may be a barrel of laughs to you, but I'm getting sick to my stomach."

"Milo told me last thing over the phone that the killer was Joe Clark." Barlowe paused for effect. Hanson didn't bat an eye. "You don't look surprised."

"I'm not."

"Maybe you're not so stupid after all."

"No. I'll give you a point there. I've been awful damn stupid."

"Clark ran him out of the file room one night when he caught him Xeroxing some papers on the Hacker. Next day Milo noticed that the Xerox counter was up twenty pages from the number he'd left it."

"So anybody could have used it."

"You sign in for it, don't you?"

"You're supposed to."

"Uh huh. Well Milo says no one had signed but yet it had been used, and the night before when Clark caught Milo he ran him out, told him he'd lock up. Know how many pages were in that file?"

"Twenty."

"Bingo. He was copying it for himself. Staying one step ahead."

"He didn't need to do that. He had access anytime he wanted. We were working on the case together."

"Good enough. But I think he wanted that material close at hand. Maybe he wanted to falsify it. I'll tell you why I'm sure he must have had ulterior motives, or rather I'll show you."

Barlowe went around to the end of the desk, stood by Hanson. He picked up the pad. "Look close." He handed it to Hanson.

Hanson took the pad and squinted his eyes. He held it beneath the desk lamp.

"That must have been the page underneath what Milo was writing. He was either finishing off his statement, or starting a new page. You can see it, can't you?"

Hanson didn't answer. He could make out most of it very well, but to be sure he put the pad on the desk and took Barlowe's pencil from him. He shaded over the indentations very carefully with the side of the pencil lead.

therefore I'm certain that the killer must be

none other than the department's own Joe Clark.

Besides the evidence already presented . . .

The rest of the writing was either too soft to have left an indentation or Milo had been cut off in mid-sentence.

"Well," Barlowe said.

"Clark's one dead sonofabitch." Hanson flashed on an image of his daughter and wife hacked to ribbons.

"He must have rigged this so as not to draw more attention to the department. If it were a Hacker murder, and the victim was a cop—"

"It would just draw more attention to him," Hanson finished.

"Looks that way to me."

"Listen. You'll get your goddamned scoop. You just drive straight to my house and tell the cops the score. There're a couple of detectives in a Volkswagen bus out front. A couple out back, and one inside. Tell them I sent you. Don't tell them I'm going to Clark's. You keep your mouth shut on that score and I'll see that you get the best interview of your life; an interview with the man that blew the Houston Hacker's brains out."

Hanson knelt down, tore the automatic from Milo's dead fingers.

"It's a deal."

"Hand me that phone book. I'm going to need Joe's address."

"Don't know your own partner's address?"

"Just give me the fuckin' phone book, Barlowe, or you get to

260

join Milo."

"No need to be testy." Barlowe picked up the telephone with his shirt tail, eased the phone book out from beneath it. He flipped it open, looked up Clark. He used the pad on the desk and his pencil that Hanson had cast aside and wrote Clark, and then under that the address.

Hanson took it, read it quickly and jammed it in his shirt pocket. He leaned over and tore the paper with Milo's fragmentary statement from the pad, and shoved it too in his shirt pocket.

"You know where I live?" Hanson asked.

"I do. It won't take me long to get there."

"Drive slow. I need all the time I can get."

"Sure."

Hanson pushed the automatic in his waistband and started out. Barlowe took a last look at Milo's body and flicked off the light.

10

It all seemed like a nightmare. Things had happened so fast Hanson had been unable to absorb the reality of it. It was as he thought, as he had deeply suspected for some time: Joe Clark was The Hacker. Joe, his partner, his friend. Could Joe be a split personality? Could one half of him be a friend, the other half a murderer? Doc Warren had suggested the possibility.

Should part of him hate Clark the fiend, another love Clark the friend? It all seemed so goddamned impossible.

But perhaps Clark knew who he was all along. Perhaps there was but one cold, calculating personality that could offer a friendly side when the need arose.

Whatever, the man had to be exterminated.

"It could be you or me," Warren had said. "It's in all of us."

Not true, Hanson told himself. And then a hard realization

came over him. If it's not true, why am I driving seventy miles an hour on a rainslick highway to blow a man's brains out without benefit of judge, jury and executioner.

No, it's true. We are all, deep down, the primeval beast, and it was far too late to change directions now.

Hanson reached Clark's apartment at 5:22 a.m. He climbed the stairs to the second level, checked the door numbers carefully. He took the automatic from his waistband and held it tightly in his hand. Just before he raised his large foot to kick in the door he thought, can I kill Joe?

The door lock gave way without a fight. Hanson hit the floor rolling, came up in darkness, his head against something hard, a table.

Nothing moved in the apartment.

His eyes accustomed themselves to the dark. Carefully he surveyed the room. He could see a bed . . . an empty bed.

He stood up slowly, half crouched.

No one jumped out to get him.

He eased back to the wall and turned on the light. He could see the kitchenette, the dining area, the bedroom-living room combination and the open door to the bathroom. He didn't see Joe.

He closed the door he had kicked open.

He checked the bathroom.

Nothing but the smell of clean towels and fresh soap lurked

in the toilet area. Somehow Hanson was surprised. He had expected the apartment to be more run-down. But it was clean, organized and fresh smelling. Even the ashtrays were empty. Joe lived in a rather run-down section of Houston, but his apartment was a nice as he could make it. An expensive stereo resided on a specially built cabinet with speakers. A color T.V. was next to that. There were rows and rows of books. And there was a desk, a typewriter on top, and a leatherbound book beside it.

Hanson put the automatic in his waistband, walked over to the desk. He picked up the book and opened it. It was a diary . . . No, it was a notebook. All of Joe's cases were listed inside, his daily routine. It wasn't exciting reading. Hanson put it aside, opened the desk drawers. Something was worrying him, something was skating precariously at the corners of his mind.

The drawers contained clippings on the Hacker. Some of them were the clippings from the station, the ones Joe had kept so long in his desk drawer. There were also clippings from *The Post* and *Chronicle*, even a brief article from *Texas Monthly* on The Hacker.

The gruesome bastard collects material pertaining to his crimes. That gave Hanson an idea. He would need it for evidence when he killed the sonofabitch, definite proof that Joe was The Hacker.

Christ! Was Joe out doing his work right now?

For a moment he shivered. Was he trying to . . . Good God! Hanson's knees trembled. Joe could come and go as he pleased. He could be at his house right now. No one would suspect his partner.

Don't panic now. Barlowe's on his way there. He knows the score. He'll inform them. If Joe's going to try that ploy they'll nab him. One man without the element of surprise can't take five.

The Volkswagen bus had curtains on the inside and special dark plastic on the windows. Anyone inside could see out. But from the outside it was impossible to see in.

Mitchel was leaning back against the bus's wall drinking a cup of lukewarm coffee. His partner, a tall, lanky man named Cramen was on watch.

"Damn Mex is gonna cost us all our jobs," Mitchel said.

"You thought it was a pretty nifty idea yourself . . . at first."

"Bullshit—"

"Hold it."

Mitchel lowered his voice. "What is it?"

"A car parked at the curb in front of the house."

Mitchel tossed off the rest of the coffee, rose up and shuffled across the bus floor on his knees. All the seats had been removed for carrying equipment, but the only equipment in it at the moment were the two cops.

They watched as the car's door opened, a small car, a Toyota maybe. It was hard to tell in the dark and the rain.

The person that got out of the car was wearing a hooded raincoat. The person walked like a man, lacked that special something a woman puts in her walk. The man was walking toward the bus and his hand was up and waving.

"He knows we're here," Mitchel said.

"Clark," Cramen said. "Got to be."

The raincoat the man was wearing was missing a button.

Hanson forced himself to go through Clark's desk drawers methodically. He found the twenty Xeroxed pages Barlowe had told him about. More evidence. He flipped through the pages. Certain items had been circled in red ink. There were several typed pages behind that, all clasped together with a paper clip.

Clark had been neatly gathering all the facts, making a case-book of them. He had drawn several conclusions and written them up in great detail.

The first one made Hanson's heart skip a beat.

Cramen opened up the sliding bus door and the man came inside with a lithe motion. Perhaps if Cramen had been watching carefully he might have seen the long blade slip down out of the raincoat sleeve and the hilt fall comfortably into The Hacker's hand. But he didn't, and he never would.

The blade made a quick silver line in the dark.

Before Cramen hit the bus floor — even before the terrible gash in his neck had time to bleed — The Hacker wheeled and brought the blade down hard and expertly on the unsuspecting Mitchel's head.

11

Clark's typed note read:

As much as I prefer to disbelieve it, the killer who calls himself The Hacker could, and I even find this hard to type, be none other than my friend and partner, Lieutenant Marvin Hanson.

Lieutenant Hanson has suffered a near nervous breakdown several times of late. His condition seems to be worsening. All this seems to have been brought on by the arrival of The Hacker murders. Often these passions, dormant since childhood, expose themselves suddenly and violently, and less often, but occasionally, the murderer is not even aware of his crimes. He lives a sort of dual existence . . .

Hanson skipped down, picked out a few sentences.

I feel certain that if Lieutenant Hanson is involved in these crimes, he is totally unaware of his dual role.

Down a little further he read:

Of course this is all hunch, and for my notes only. At least until I can prove something. If there's anything to be proved. I certainly hope not. I feel like a traitor just thinking such thoughts, even if it is merely to myself.

Hanson stood dumbfounded for a moment. My God, he thought, Joe thinks The Hacker might be me.

The Hacker wiped his blade clean of blood on Cramen's pants leg. He did this slowly and methodically, allowing his nostrils to fill with the sexually arousing scent of blood. Then he opened the door to the bus and slipped out into the wet night.

He slid the door back into position, hoping there would be time to work on the bodies later. Of course if he could get to the women, well . . . there was nothing like women.

He slid the bayonet back up his sleeve, and walked casually across the street toward the back of the house.

Hanson flipped a few pages. Joe kept this typed record as a supplement to his diary. The organization showed there was still much of the student in Clark. I never really knew him, Hanson concluded.

He found more pages listing suspects. Former sex offenders and brutal murderers. They got less than a paragraph apiece. God! He was Joe's prime suspect. The last page was devoted to another suspect. No real evidence, just suspicions. And now, knowing what he knew, Hanson realized that this one was the right one.

Hanson pulled the paper Milo had left his written indentations on out of his pocket. He put the address Barlowe had written for him beside it. The writing on the two pieces of paper matched up. They had been done by the same man. It had all been an elaborate plant.

No two ways about it. The Hacker had to be . . .

12

"Barlowe!"

The two policemen had approached the raincoated figure from opposite sides, guns drawn.

Barlowe had made no effort to conceal himself. In fact he made it easy, he had pulled back his hood.

The burly cop who had spoken before said, "Whaterya doing here?"

"Paper. Reporter on the ball," Barlowe said, grinning.

The other cop, wearing a slicker like his partner, but hoodless, said, "We almost blew your fuckin' head off."

"I heard you had a little party planned for The Hacker."

"You just get your ass outta here . . . How'd you know about this?" the burly cop asked.

"Like I always know," Barlowe rubbed his thumb and fingers together, "contacts."

"Well," the hoodless cop said, "you best make contact and get outta here."

"Okay, already," Barlowe said . . . "You guys wouldn't want to make some money?"

The burly cop said, "You wouldn't be suggesting a bribe to a police officer, would you?"

"Not me," Barlowe said. "Just know where you guys might get a part-time job."

"Guy's a million laughs," the burly cop said.

"You got a minute to beat it," the bare-headed cop said.

The cops put their guns away, walked up close to Barlowe. Very close. "You deaf," the hoodless cop said. "Go."

"Sure," Barlowe said.

Barlowe let the bayonet slide down out of his sleeve and into his hand.

"Hey," the burly cop said. "What ya got . . . "

Barlowe clamped his free left hand over the hoodless cop's right hand and, slashing out at the other cop, struck him in the temple. The burly cop stumbled back, wobbled, fell to his knees. His hands went to his head but he was dead before they touched. He fell forward in the grass.

The hoodless cop jerked his hand free of Barlowe's grasp, went for the gun in his shoulder holster.

Barlowe slashed the cop's hand off at the wrist. Kicked him in the groin, and then with a Muskateer lunge, ran the bayonet through the cop's heart.

The cop went down spurting blood from his wrist and chest, the momentum of his backwards falling body allowing Barlowe to jerk the blade back in one smooth motion.

Maybe, thought Barlowe, I was a little crazy to try that.

But since nobody shot at him, he figured he was almost home free. Of course there was bound to be someone in the house.

Barlowe crept quietly around the house 'til he found the fuse box. He opened it and went to work.

Inside, Martinez didn't realize he no longer had electricity. He was worried sick about Hanson . . . Worried more about his ass. Something like this could lose him his job.

In less than twenty minutes he would lose his life.

13

Martinez answered the knock at the front door with his service revolver drawn. He left the night-chain in place, peeked out at the drenched form of Barlowe.

He thought, why in hell isn't that fool wearing his hood? He said, "Aren't you that reporter?"

"Yep."

"How'd you get wind of this—"

"Come on, your buddies said you'd let me in."

"They did, did they?"

"That's right."

"This is one hell of a stake-out."

"For goodness sake, let me get in out of this rain. Who the hell you think I am, The Hacker?"

Martinez hesitated. He'd made one fuck up tonight. That was bad enough. Two wasn't going to help any.

"I think you should take a hike, and tell Mitchel . . . Was it Mitchel?"

"Yeah, Mitchel."

". . . Well tell him to suck an egg."

"Come on, man. Hanson sent me."

"Hanson."

"Yeah. I told Mitchel. He said you'd let me in."

"Where is Hanson?"

"Collaring The Hacker, that's where."

"Well I'll be damned. That lying sonofa . . . "

Martinez slipped off the night-chain. When Barlowe lunged he still had his gun in his hand, but the blade came so quick he never thought to use it.

14

With trembling fingers Hanson dialed his home number.

The phone began to ring the minute Martinez hit the floor.
Barlowe listened.
One ring.
Two rings.
Three rings.
Four rings.
He heard a car drive up the driveway.
That's five rings, thought Hanson, Martinez will answer now.
He didn't.
The phone rang again.

Rachel counted the rings. Six. Why in the hell didn't Marvin answer the phone?

The phone rang a seventh time.

Joe Clark got out of his car and slipped on his raincoat. The rain was coming down hard and fast now. The trees and shrubs whipped to the tune of frequent thunder and flashing lightning.

Clark started across the street for the bus at a run.

The Hacker, out in the night, his hood pulled up now, became the hunter once again.

On the ninth ring Rachel couldn't stand it anymore. She answered.

"Rachel!" Hanson said. "Where's Martinez?"

"Marve . . . What . . . I thought you were downstairs."

"No time to explain. Please listen. Now try to stay as calm as you can. Barlowe is the man."

"The man — The Hacker?"

"Yes."

"I don't understand."

"I'm afraid he may be in the house with you."

Rachel made a little strangled sound of fear.

"Lock the door," Hanson said, "and I'm on my way. I'll call

the station, get the law moving."

"Hurry, Marve."

"I'm gone, honey."

Hanson slammed down the phone, darted out of Joe's apartment, went down the stairs taking them two at a time.

15

Clark found the bodies in the bus. He stared at them for a long, hard moment.

"Gorilla," he said aloud. "My God."

He drew his revolver and turned.

Barlowe, quiet as the falling of the dew, was on him.

Clark never knew what hit him.

Rachel locked the bedroom door, pulled a chair over and against it; propped it so that the back was lodged firmly beneath the doorknob.

Next she tried to wake JoAnna.

No dice. The sedatives were too strong.

She quit tugging at JoAnna's unconscious form and went to the closet. She opened the door, moved items from the closet floor, stuck them in the shelf above. She went back to JoAnna, and by placing her hands beneath JoAnna's armpits, dragged the girl from the bed and onto the floor. JoAnna's heels clunked loudly.

Rachel held her breath for a moment. She didn't hear any movement.

She dragged JoAnna to the closet and managed her inside. Placed her so that her knees were drawn up and JoAnna was leaning her side against the closet wall.

Very gently, she kissed her baby on the cheek, then stood and closed the closet door.

Hanson got the speedometer up to one-twenty, nearly lost it several times. The rain blasted his windshield. The tires refused to grab properly. He dropped it down to eighty regretfully, reached over and clutched his radio mike to call in the police; comrades in arms.

The speaker wire was cut.

Rachel went back to where she had left her hammer, next to the phone. She wasn't going to do anything foolish, like hide under the bed or in the half-bath. She was going to give the sonofabitch hell. He hadn't seen resistance 'til he saw a mother bear fight to protect her cub.

The hammer felt good in her hand.

Real good.

✦   ✦   ✦

The sonofabitch cut the wire when he was pretending to drop his cigarettes, Hanson concluded. The wiley, motherfucking sonofabitch. He could stop and call the law. That might be what he should do. But the car's momentum, the rushing of the little white and yellow highway snakes beneath his automobile, gave him a feeling of progress. He felt that if he slowed down no one would be there on time. Not the police. Not him.

Tricky bastard, thought Hanson. He must have thought Milo was getting wise, killed him and his family off and took advantage of the situation to lure me out of the house. Or maybe he just used Milo because he was handy and he could paint a good picture around his family's death.

"Fool, fool," Hanson said aloud and pounded his fist on the dash 'til it hurt and he nearly lost control of the rocketing automobile.

He was on a straitaway now. The Houston Ship Channel Bridge was coming up.

No place to stop and phone 'til he was on the other side of the bridge and several miles down the road. By then he'd be less than twenty-five miles away.

The highway was wide. Visibility with the bridge and highway lights was good, so . . .

Hanson put the pedal to the floor. Passed the only vehicle on the road; a slow moving cattle truck whisking its sour cattle-pie odor to the night wind.

By the time he crossed the bridge and took the Pasadena exit he was doing a hundred miles an hour. The exit sign said thirty-five miles per hour.

Barlowe put Clark's body in the bus with the other two and went back to the house.

Inside he began to call, "Oh niggers, come out, come out wherever you are."

Rachel stiffened. Her throat felt dry. Her hand cramped on the hammer handle. "Come and get it you sonofabitch," she said beneath her breath, and she moved toward the door.

On the straightaway Hanson reached one hundred-twenty miles per hour. The car was rocking side to side, making a sound like bowling balls knocking together.

"Tire don't blow now," Hanson said between gritted teeth. "Stay with me baby."

The railing posts just looked like dots.

Rachel heard footsteps on the stairs.

Thump, thump, thump, climbing very slowly.

It was all she could do not to jerk the chair out of the way and pull the door open, go down after that sonofabitch.

She reached out and took hold of the chair.

No. Don't be a goddamned fool. That's just what he wants.

She could hear the footsteps better now. He was nearing the top of the stairs.

After a moment the steps stopped.

He was on the landing.

Where are all the cops when you need them? thought Hanson wryly. The same complaint had been handed to him many times, and it always made him mad. Now he wanted to know the answer.

Here he was doing one-twenty on a rain-slicked highway and not a traffic cop in sight.

He began rocking forward, pushing at the wheel, as if by sheer physical effort he could manage more speed.

The voice was very close.

"Oh niggers, come out, come out wherever your black, shiny asses are."

Rachel listened with her ear to the door. The voice went down the hall repeating the chant. He was checking the rooms one by one. And this one was the last one.

He was eating up the miles now.

Ten.
Nine.
Eight.

Barlowe was at her door now.

"Oh niggers, I know you're in there."

Barlowe took hold of the doorknob, shook it.

"Might as well let me in, niggers. I'm going to get in anyway. I like black pussy, niggers. It's all pink on the inside, you know."

Barlowe laughed. It was a madman's laugh.

"Then maybe you don't know, but I'll show you your insides. Won't that be fun?"

He laughed again.

"Well, for me anyway."

Rachel began to tremble as she moved back from the door. If she could just get in one good lick, right between the eyes.

Suddenly a silver tongue of metal slammed through the door.

Six miles.
Five.

Hanson forced himself to slow it to fifty. The streets were too narrow. Too wet.

Four.

288

A corner was coming up.

He tried to take it at fifty.

The car whipped, the rearend slammed against a telephone pole, spun into the middle of the road, then, whirling like a dervish, it crossed to the right side of the road, slammed hard against the curb and flipped.

The bayonet came through the door time after time. The shining point of the blade seemed to point at Rachel.

Slamming it through the wood with both hands, grunting with the effort, Barlowe was working himself up to a frenzy.

When he had splintered the wood well enough for him to see inside, he leaned forward for a peek.

Even in the dark, Rachel could see the eyes. Cold. Merciless. Glazed with lust.

"I'm coming for you, nigger," Barlowe said hoarsely. "You might as well spread 'em and get ready."

"Come and try, you honkey motherfucker, come and try."

The car rocked on its top and settled. Hanson crawled out through the window, made it shakily to his feet.

Lights in houses across the street went on.

Hanson sprinted for the nearest one.

The blade went to work again, a hungry tongue lapping up wood. The blade slammed, screeched as Barlowe withdrew it for another strike. A hole as big as a man's head appeared, and Barlowe's hand snaked in for the lock, encountered the chair. He grabbed it and tugged it from beneath the doorknob. It rattled to the floor.

Now the lock was easy to get at. He worked it with his thumb. It snickered free.

"Police officer," Hanson yelled. "Open the goddamned door."

A middle aged man in pajamas and robe answered the door. Hanson flashed his wallet and shield at him.

"What seems to be the matter, offic—"

"Your car. I've got to have it, this is an emergency."

"Well, I don't . . . "

Hanson grabbed the man by the collar of his robe and slammed him against the door sill. "Your car keys, you fuckin' moron. This is life or death."

The man started shaking his head. "I'll get them. I'll get them."

Hanson let go of the man and he disappeared inside, came back with the keys. "It's in the garage," the man said.

"Open it."

"All right. Take it easy." The man's eyes had rested on the automatic in Hanson's belt. He was beginning to think he had a maniac impersonating a police officer on his hands. He opened the garage.

"A Volkswagen?" Hanson said.

"That's it," the man said apologetically. "Good gas mileage . . ."

"The bike," Hanson said motioning to a Harley Davidson close to the garage wall, "does it run?"

"Sure, but that's my son's . . ."

Hanson took out the automatic.

"But I know right where the keys are," the man said quickly.

The man went inside to get them with Hanson close on his heels.

When the door slammed back and Rachel saw the bayonet in Barlowe's hand she knew real fear. Stark, crazy fear.

She ran directly for him, bringing the hammer down with all the strength in her lithe body.

It was a good blow. There was plenty of shoulder and hip in it, and had it connected, it would surely have killed Barlowe.

Had it connected.

It didn't.

Barlowe caught the hammer head with the flat of his blade and flicked it out of Rachel's hand. It flew across the room and struck her dressing table, knocking over the sack of nails and several bottles of cosmetics.

Barlowe reached out and took Rachel by the neck, clutched

'til the wind died in her throat and her eyes bulged. Eyes just like a Chihuahua dog he had butchered once. Just like that.

He bent his arm and shoved her back as hard as he could. She crashed to the floor in a heap.

He walked over to her, took her by the hair and pulled her up to her knees.

"You bitch. Tried to hit me with a hammer, did you? I'm going to show you what it's like, bitch. You hear me, bitch?"

He shook her head violently.

"On your feet, bitch. You and all women. Bitches, bitches, bitches."

He tugged at her hair, jerking out a handful by the roots.

"Up," he screamed, and he buried his fingers in her hair again. He tugged her to her feet, pushed her back against the wall and held her there with one hand, raised the bayonet with the other and brought it crashing down into the wall beside her.

He left the blade sticking in the wall, quivering with the force of his thrust.

"You thought that was it, didn't you, nigger?"

Rachel just looked at him, her eyes wide, her mouth trembling.

"Not that easy, sister, not that easy."

He grabbed her by the hair again and slung her down hard at his feet. He reached over to the dresser and picked up the hammer.

And then he saw the nails and had a better idea.

He hadn't been on a bike in years. His handling of it was a little off, but he was managing.

Less than a mile now. The rain was dying. Visibility was good.

He gave it full throttle.

Half a mile.

"Come on, baby," Hanson said to the Harley, "eat the road."

Two blocks now and closing.

Barlowe pulled Rachel up against the wall again. The flimsy nightgown she was wearing came open, revealed her breast. Barlowe grinned, squeezed it, pinched the nipple.

Rachel spit in his face.

Barlowe jerked his head back and frowned.

"Go right ahead, nigger. It just makes it that much more fun for me."

He held the hammer in his free hand. He let go of her and crashed his fist into her face.

Rachel's head slammed against the wall. She began to slide down, but Barlowe pushed his hip into her, held her up. He took her right hand and opened it, pulled her arm out to its full length, then holding her in place with his hip, he took one of the nails he had put in his pocket and placed it in the center of her palm.

Then, holding it in place with his left hand, he began to drive the nail with the hammer in his right.

Hanson skidded into the yard and dropped the bike. He rolled head over heels in the grass, scraped against the driveway for a mild case of asphalt rash. In an instant he was on his feet, darting for the front door.

He had just discovered the door unlocked when Rachel screamed.

16

Consciousness, like a hateful imp, returned to Rachel the moment the nail went through her palm into the wall. The slim nail hurt tremendously, but the head of the hammer smashing her palm sent shockwaves of unbearable pain throughout her body.

Rachel struggled.

Barlowe, his lips peeled back to expose the gums, took her other hand and forced it out against the wall.

Rachel closed her hand, scraped at his wrist and fingers with her long nails. She leaned out from the wall and tried to bite him.

He was just about to manage to get the nail in place when he heard a crash from below.

When Hanson heard the screams he pushed the door back and rushed in . . . and tripped over Martinez's body.

He scrambled to his feet and tried the light switch.

Click. Nothing. No lights.

He started for the stairs at a run.

Barlowe let go of Rachel and dropped the hammer. He jerked the bayonet from the wall and started for the bedroom door.

"Just hang tight, nigger, I'll be back."

He went out to the landing and started down the stairs.

Hanson was three steps up when he saw Barlowe.

"Greetings," Barlowe said. "Let me introduce myself." Barlowe had adopted a Bela Lugosi accent. "I am The Houston Hacker."

Hanson reached for the gun in his belt.

It wasn't there.

A feeling of unreality swept over Hanson. He must have lost it when he dropped the bike.

Barlowe was coming down the stairs, waving the bayonet.

"I want to see your blood," Barlowe said, still affecting the Lugosi accent. Then in his own voice, made hoarse by excitement, "I should have killed you earlier, nigger."

"Why didn't you?" Hanson said, thinking about Martinez. Maybe he had a gun on him. And maybe not. He didn't want to expose his back to find out.

"Too much fun watching you suffer, watching you go after your partner. Too bad you didn't find him. But I did. He's headed for his last roundup, Rastus. And you my black-faced wide-eyed Al Jolson, have eaten your last crispy fried chicken."

With that Barlowe lept forward, covered three stair steps.

The blade was a whistling flash of light as it reached for Hanson's gut.

Hanson leaned back, an involuntary, "Uhh," came from his throat.

The blade came back for him, like a falcon that had missed its prey on the first dive.

Hanson leapt to the right, fell back against the stair rail.

The bayonet cut only wind again.

Barlowe, grunting now with effort and anger, came for Hanson again, and this time the hungry blade found food. It sliced through his coat, shirt and the flesh on his side. Hanson could feel the blood run wet and warm.

The blade was not content with coat, shirt and flesh, it continued to travel, struck one of the stair rail rungs and sliced it where it connected to the top rail. The blow was so vicious the bottom portion of the rung came unlodged halfway.

Hanson dove for Barlowe's legs before he could bring the blade back for another taste of flesh. The attack knocked the madman's feet out from under him and drove him back against the opposite rail.

Barlowe didn't drop the blade. He struck down with it, but lying as he was, his head full of dizzy bees, he could only strike the huge black man with the hilt behind the right ear.

Once.

Twice.

Hanson rolled to his left.

Barlowe struck out at Hanson with the bayonet. Hanson

caught Barlowe's wrist, but lying on his back, the madman now firmly on top, he could feel his grip lessening.

The blade seemed very, very close to his face.

Hanson kicked up between Barlowe's legs, smashed him in the groin, and with his free hand, tried to dig out the butcher's eyes. Hanson raised his foot again. The kick to the groin had had little or no effect. This time he pushed instead of kicked, planted his foot in Barlowe's groin and just shooooooooved.

Barlowe went up and back.

Hanson scrambled to his feet.

Barlowe had come up like a cat. He slashed hard and fast at Hanson, trying to slice him into black ribbons.

Most of the slashes were wild, but the narrow stairway offered few places to hide. One blow hit Hanson in the left shoulder and cut to the bone. Blood sprayed both of the men, and Hanson felt the shock of the blade to his toes. A wave of blackness swept over him like an incoming tide, but he fought it, forced it back to sea.

No matter, thought Hanson, it's all over now.

He had just enough energy to move away from a wild downward cut. He pushed both palms against Barlowe's side, wheeled around him and collapsed against the railing on the other side. Instinctively he brought his hand up to his face, to protect against the blade . . . and his fingers touched something sharp.

The fingers told his brain that he had touched the broken stair railing.

Hanson clamped his hand around it, jerked it free.

Barlowe, grinning, struck the coup de grace.

Or so he thought.

Hanson kicked out with his left leg, struck Barlowe's right knee cap. The knee made a cracking sound.

The force of his downward swing, coupled with the weakened knee, carried Barlowe forward, off target. The bayonet ate through half the stair rail, lodged.

Barlowe tugged at the blade, brought it free.

Hanson raised up and slammed the wooden stake into Barlowe with every ounce of strength left in his body.

The stake penetrated Barlowe's chest on the left side. Blood sprinkled around the stake, splashed Hanson with red hot jewels, and then with a rushing scarlet flood.

Barlowe tried to straighten, but instead he went forward over the rail. As he fell, he thought in the dim recesses of his brain, he had seen his own blood, and it had been . . . *beautiful*.

Barlowe struck the floor with a thud and the bayonet fell across his body like a cross. The hilt beneath his chin, the blade pointing down.

Hanson, black dots swarming before his eyes like bacteria beneath a microscope, pulled off his jacket and pressed it to his wound, started up the stairs, half walking, half stumbling.

A pencil of light stabbed through the window below, touched Barlowe's dead face with the first gentle kiss of dawn.

EPILOGUE

Jack the Ripper's dead.
And lying on his bed.
He cut his throat
With Sunlight soap.
Jack the Ripper's dead.
    — *Children's chant from the East End of London*

THREE DAYS LATER

Joe Clark's funeral put the period on Hanson's cop career.

When the last sod was thrown, Hanson, his arm around Rachel, JoAnna walking solemnly by his side, started for the cemetery gate. Rachel's right hand was in a partial cast — several small bones in her hand, broken by the hammer. They were almost to the gate when a small, white-haired man walked up to meet them, Doc Warren.

"I'm afraid I missed the funeral," Doc Warren said.

"It was very nice," Rachel said and began to cry.

"Take your mother down to the car," Hanson said to JoAnna.

JoAnna took Rachel by the arm and led her out of the gate and to the car.

"Something I said?" Doc Warren asked.

Hanson smiled. "No. Just been through a lot."

Doc Warren nodded. "How's your shoulder?"

Hanson looked down at the sling that held his left arm. "All right, as long as I don't move it much.'

"You're leaving, aren't you?" Doc Warren said.

"I am."

"We'll be losing a good cop."

"No, you won't. I've been very stupid and very incompetent. Joe Clark was a far better cop than I ever was. I'm something else inside, not a cop."

"Anybody can suffer emotional strain."

Hanson touched Doc Warren on the shoulder. "Thanks. But I don't want to chance it again. Stupidity almost cost me my family."

"Not stupidity."

"Whatever. I did learn one thing, Doc. You were right. The killer is in all of us, each and every one of us."

"How do you feel . . . about Barlowe?"

"Glad that I could protect my family, but sad. Not satisfied like I thought I'd be. Something's missing in me."

Warren nodded. "I was in the war. I still think about it."

"You killed?"

Warren nodded.

"Did you feel hollow inside?"

"I did, and it doesn't go away. I wish I could tell you it does, but it doesn't . . . But in time you do learn to cope with it."

"I hope so . . . I've got to go now."

"Don't make yourself a stranger, hear?"

"I hear," Hanson said, and he held out his hand.

They shook and Hanson walked down to the car.

AFTERWORD

AFTERWORD

Joe R. Lansdale

In the Fall of 1979, at the age of 27, soon to be 28, I realized I was spinning my wheels as a writer. I had written a number of published short stories and articles, none that were particularly special, and I had written several novels, none that were particularly special, and fortunately, none that had sold.

I thought one of them, a private eye novel based on a character, Ray Slater, I created for *Mike Shayne Mystery Magazine* was pretty good, good enough to publish, but nothing to get excited about, and frankly, I didn't like that. I was doing the best I could at the time, and had nothing to feel bad about. I wasn't slacking, I was learning. But that didn't make me feel all that good about being able to write a novel that was only so-so.

A certain attitude was growing inside me, one that told me I was better than what I was doing, and by that, I don't mean better than the material, but that I could personally perform better.

I felt I needed to readjust my thinking cap, tilt that sucker a bit to the left, or push it back on my head. I was in the rut of recreating what had gone before. The same old private eye and western stories, same old science fiction adventures.

In time, a publisher needing something of that sort, a rack filler, would probably land on one of my books and pay me a piddling sum and it would be published. But getting published was no longer my main goal. I wanted that. But I wanted something else. Inside I was stirring. I actually felt I had a voice, but I was wearing a mute. I needed to take it off and talk my way.

I was beginning to feel more comfortable with dialogue and my East Texas background was seeping more and more into my work. *Act of Love* doesn't show those elements as much as my later work, but the vestiges of those things are there, and I feel that this book, better or worse, is the one that actually made me a writer. It has influences, and like my short stories of this period, they are more obvious than now. The influences were Evan Hunter, writing both under that name and Ed McBain, Dean Koontz, mostly the work he wrote as Brian Coffey, John Ball, Richard Matheson, and numerous crime and pulp writers, but I was also there. I didn't feel that I was writing a book anyone else could write. Someone could have taken the same basic story and written an acceptable novel from it, but there was something about the book that was all mine. An attitude, a personal flair.

Looking back, I'd have to say the main nod to Texas in *Act of Love* is the location. But even this was something a bit bothersome to New York publishers at the time, if some of the rejects and comments I got from editors are to be believed.

Back then, New York and Los Angeles thought they were the world. They still do, but the rest of the country no longer lets them believe that in peace. Writers, primarily those designated as genre writers, who wrote about the South, or Texas, were considered regional. This was a nice way of saying "hick" and "stupid." And the general wisdom was no one wanted to read about that sort of thing.

But I refused to be brow beat. I still wanted to write a crime novel and I wanted to use Texas as the background. Back then, I felt it essential I have a big city as a backdrop, so I chose Houston. That's one of the novel's weaknesses. Houston is written about, but it's written about by a small town and country boy who hates it, and really doesn't know much about it, except that when he's there he's irritated and depressed. It's worse than New York in some ways, because it lacks the glamour that New York can occasionally achieve if the sun's shining just right and the wind is blowing the stench of garbage and piss in a direction opposite you and you're in a good mood.

But, to be generous, if New York's a shit hole, Houston is two shit holes, though I admit to feeling somewhat safer in Houston, which may have more to do with my understanding Southerners better than Northerners.

Still, I took Houston as my background. At least it was Texas, and it opened my head to a new way of thinking. I was coming close to the Hemingway credo: "Write what you know."

Backtrack a bit. At the same time I was considering a new novel, but hadn't quite grasped the subject matter for it, my wife was attending the University here in Nacogdoches, finishing up her degree in criminology. She offered me her books and papers to read, and one of the books she was reading was Fromm's *The Anatomy of Human Destructiveness*. Grim business. One of the papers she had written was on the book. I read the paper, her evaluation of the subject matter, then read the book. Both paper and book, of course, dealt with the dark side of human nature, and that dark side was so dark as to contain no sunrise. For that matter, there was no moon and no stars, just an absence of light.

The book and her paper intrigued and horrified me. It went along with all the horrible crimes I was reading about in the newspapers. Crimes only hinted at when I was a child, back when Richard Speck and Charles Whitman were news not only because of what they had done, but because such a thing was considered so rare and improbable. Jack the Ripper began to seem very minor league after those guys and their "disciples." The world became somewhat more frightening to me. I lost my attitude that everyone deserves to live. Assholes like that, who do those sort of things, for whatever reason, they deserve to go. A cancer is doing what a cancer knows to do, but that doesn't mean if I had one growing in me I wouldn't want it cut out. I feel the same about serial killers and their ilk. They're a cancer, and they need to go.

Random violence became my greatest fear. I have seen a bit of it in my time, on a small scale. Sudden, unprovoked violence from individuals who viewed it as a kind of entertainment, but nothing of the sort the U.S. as a whole was experiencing. There seemed to be some great social mutation going on. As if nature was trying to devise population control by installing a self-destruct factor into human beings, making certain human beings hit men against their own kind.

I believe a person's childhood and culture affects what they become, but I also believe genetics plays a greater role in all this than we like to admit. That scares me even more. Andrew Vachss says: "There's no biogenetic code for serial killers or rapists—we make our own monsters.".

No one I respect more than Andrew Vachss, and I agree with this statement. I believe we all have a dark side and it can be brought to the surface at times. But I also believe some folks are born with certain factors missing; factors that leave them in the dark. It's not a matter of having a code for such things, it's a lack of empathy and nothing can awaken empathy in such an individual. I believe empathy is inborn, even if it has to be awakened. It's built into human beings as part of the survival factor. Fucking and eating just aren't enough to explain the continuance of humanity. But in the same way that some people are born with greater muscle tone than others, some are born with less empathy than others. Or a lesser ability to have this empathy awakened.

One factor that makes me believe this is observation. Even though some criminals are made, there are those individuals who've had horrible lives and similar experiences to certain "made" criminals who don't become horrible because of it. So how much does genetics weigh? What about free will? What's the real scoop?

What do we do if some criminals *are* born and not made? Or

to be more precise, what if they are born *to be made*? What if the genetics and the background are both negative factors? What if no matter what society does, no matter what sort of childhoods these individuals experience, they're going to gravitate towards a certain type of behavior? That of the predators.

I asked myself these questions, read every book I could get my hands on that dealt with the subject, and let it all boil. I didn't really come up with any answers, other than the general one I've already offered, and I admit it's up for debate, but I did come up with a lot of speculation. Stuff that stimulated and intrigued me as a writer.

Finally, I began to write. The book went well and quickly for several months in 1980, but it wore on me. All that research into darkness, all the dark dreams I was having, the fact that I was getting in touch with the dark side of my nature, and realizing we all have that dark side, was very disturbing. A rare mood of depression descended on me. I suppose, I was for the first time really becoming an adult.

After a break of a couple of months or so to put some light back into my head, I returned to the novel and re-read it. Thought, "You know, this ain't bad."

I concluded it was powerful and fast paced with a good mystery, and at the time, I felt it was pretty well-written. It was also very graphic. Just the way the crimes I read about were graphic. I had used actual crimes and their descriptions to write my novel. The violence may seem over the top — especially then — but it was very much based on reality. Not something that was proper in "mainstream" mystery suspense books then, or horror books for that matter. Least not to that degree. That sort of thing was frowned upon.

I had encountered it in certain books, series like *The Gladiator*, which was as the title suggests, about a Roman gladiator and his adventures, and I had read some *Edge* books, which were bloody, parody Westerns, but there was little else of this nature about, and none of these books seemed to be using violence to any real end, other than to move the story and titillate, or as a sort of bloody, cartoonish comedy. Acceptable reasons, perhaps, but for me, not enough of a reason.

I felt I could use the graphic elements to my advantage. I felt in my youthful enthusiasm, I could do all of the above and more. I was of the opinion my approach was something special, and that my voice was coming through, and that unlike *The Gladiator* and *Edge*, I really had some thematic point to make, was touching on modern society, the change from a fifties mentality to one that was darker and sadder and scarier.

I didn't believe I was trivilizing violence, but I was aware of its natural hooking power, and I felt I was attempting to look violence in the face and see it as it really was.

After reading what I had written, I decided it was time to finish up. Next day — one long and rare and glorious day, from early in the morning until two the next morning (guess that actually makes it a bit longer than one day) — I wrote the last third of the book, a third which later needed very little revising.

Now, I might feel differently about that revising, and might do more on the entire book, but I truly believe it was the best I could do at the time.

When I stood up at two thirty a.m. I was on fire with excitement. I had written the book, and I was pleased. I knew it was good. I knew it was different. Most of the time I don't know how I feel about a project when finished, but I was young enough then to think I had done a special job, and frankly, taking into consideration the times in which the book was written, my level of skill then, I still feel that way. It's not quite the wonderment I thought it was that morning at two thirty some twelve years ago, but it still beats stepping on a tack or being butt-fucked by a nearsighted rhino.

I sent the book to my then agent, who was unreliable and quarrelsome, and she thought I had a hit. She went nuts for it. She had big plans. She was going to put it up for auction. It was going to be a bestseller.

Wrong.

It went to every publisher in the business. Some of them twice. The agent began to think it wasn't a bestseller. She began to suggest I write like certain other authors.

The rejects ranged from cries of abomination to raves. But the raves didn't help. Editors said how much they loved it, but truly believed buying the book would get them fired or looked down on by their peers, and one editor even said I was genius and that I was ahead of my time. I liked that last one for about five minutes. A reject is a reject, friends, and the word genius is used these days about as freely as the words cholesterol and breast cancer. The latter two exist, genius is a little harder to measure.

Another editor suggested I change my black protagonist to a white protagonist, and then the book would take off.

All of this, to say the least, left me a little disappointed. I also began to notice that the movies were moving in a direction that was more graphic. I felt this was a road sign of things to come in publishing. (It works both ways. Movies influence books. Books influence movies.) I had my finger on the pulse of things after all, but I was beginning to think it didn't matter. I figured by the time the book was published, *Act of Love* would be old hat. If it were published at all.

Finally, my agent in a last ditch measure, sent it to Zebra Books. Zebra sprang for the book in the Fall of Eighty and it came out early Eighty-one. I was paid a very decent advance for a first novel, and made some royalties, got some good reviews, upset some people, and was refused rack space by some bookstores on the basis of content. I gave myself a present after the sale of the book. I fired my agent and moved on to a series of incompetents and unsuitables in that profession until I hitched up with the Peekner Agency a few years later and began once again to write books. I'm still writing books. I'm still with the Peekner Agency.

Since the book's publication, it has, considering it's humble origins, done well. It's been reprinted in paper by Zebra, and this is it's second hardback appearance.

How do I feel about the book? How does it stand up?

I think the editor who called me a genius was right. Not about the genius part. But the other part—that the book was ahead of its time. I'm not saying it's the only book that addressed this sort of thing early on, since *Psycho* and many fine, and better books, were before it, but it was one of the first to use its dark subject matter in such a graphic manner. It was a pioneer there. The graphic nature of the book is its heart and the violence comes across as grim and informed and experimental, if a little exploitive. In one sense, violence and sex are always exploitive, no matter what the intent. But it is the intent that counts, and I believe my intentions were good.

Now there's blood and gore in everything, and it's used on the same level as nudity and brand names and has about as much resonance as disco music. A technique that works once or twice doesn't necessarily work every time out, and since that time I've varied my arsenal.

I believe *Act of Love* still has power and pace and a good story, but, alas, it's more purple and desperate than I realized. It's not quite the great social tract-ala-entertainment I thought it to be originally, though that element is there. It reads as if it were written by another Joe R. Lansdale. A twenty-nine year old janitor struggling to break free of blue collar jobs, charging up against a blank page with blind confidence and determination.

It was a melding of mystery, suspense, horror, social commentary, B movies, police procedural, and pulp into a concoction that was then truly unique.

I honestly believe that books like *The Silence of the Lambs* and *Red Dragon* flowed in its wake and the wake of similar material, and the influence of films. I'm not saying my book was read by Thomas

Harris and it inspired him. I'm not saying mine is better or as good as his. It's not. I know that. But I think *Act of Love* was one of the starting shots for a lot of books and films that came after. Some of those changes good, some not so good.

Would this change in fiction have happened without *Act of Love*?

Of course. I just happened to be there. And there were the films. They influenced too. There were also other writers. It was time.

But still, I was there at the time of the sea change, was one of those riding the waves, and it was exciting. I'm also pleased at the number of new writers who tell me *Act of Love* was the book that turned them around. Got them excited about writing, about charging into their subject matter with all guns blazing. That's a pretty special achievement by itself.

All right. I'll leave you to the book and to your own evaluations. I'm a little embarrassed to have carried on like this, but that's what an *Afterword* is about. I'll close with this. I hope you enjoy it, and be gentle, it's my first. Lastly, I hope the checks you've written to purchase it don't bounce so CD Publications will get their money and I'll get my cut.

Happy trails. Happy sidewalks.

And may there be no dark moments in your life.

—Joe R. Lansdale
August 1992